ZANE PRESENTS

RECKONING

THE KINK, P.I. SERIES: BOOK 3

Dear Reader:

Shakir Rashaan introduced readers to his brand of erotica with his Chronicles of the Nubian Underworld series. A practitioner of Atlanta's BDSM and Fetish community, the author offers a real-life portrayal of this world in his works.

His Kink, P.I. series continues with *Reckoning*, the third installment. The debonair detective Dominic Law returns to solve a couple of gruesome murders, including one that hits close to home. Along his trail, he encounters a nemesis, who places his own life in danger as well as those he holds dear. Sit back and enjoy the suspenseful ride brimming with Dominant/submissive relationships and love triangles. With the story's many twists, subplots and surprises, readers will keep guessing the identity of the culprits.

To find out how it all starts with Detective Law, check out the excerpt in the back of this book from *Obsession*, Book One in the Kink, P.I. series.

As always, thanks for supporting myself and the Strebor Books family. We strive to bring you the most cutting-edge, out-of-the-box material on the market. You can find me on Facebook @AuthorZane or you can email me at zane@eroticanoir.com.

Blessings,

Zane

Publisher
Strebor Books
www.simonandschuster.com

ZANE PRESENTS

RECKONING

THE KINK, P.I. SERIES: BOOK 3

A NOVEL

SHAKIR RASHAAN

SBI

STREBOR BOOKS

NEW YORK LONDON TORONTO SYDNEY

Strebor Books
P.O. Box 6505
Largo, MD 20792
www.simonandschuster.com

ISBN 978-1-59309-606-9
ISBN 978-1-4767-7597-5 (ebook)
LCCN 2015957695

First Strebor Books trade paperback edition June 2016

Cover design: www.mariondesigns.com
Cover photograph: © Keith Saunders/Keith Saunders Photos

10 9 8 7 6 5 4 3 2 1

Manufactured in the United States of America

For information regarding special discounts for bulk purchases, please contact Simon & Schuster Special Sales at 1-866-506-1949

The Simon & Schuster Speakers Bureau can bring authors to your live event. For more information or to book an event, contact the Simon & Schuster Speakers Bureau at 1-866-248-3049 or visit our website at www.simonspeakers.com.

Vengeance is in my heart,
Death in my hand,
Blood and revenge are hammering in my head.
—*William Shakespeare*

For my Beloved...
It sounds like I'm repeating myself,
but it never gets old when I say it...
You are, and always will be,
the best thing that has ever happened to me.
I love you.

ACKNOWLEDGMENTS

This never gets old...six books and counting, and it feels like the first time every time!

Let's get the particulars out of the way, shall we?

Unlike my Nubian Underworld series, these books are a complete work of fiction, although I have taken some stories that are pertinent to what I wanted to bring to light in that moment, and *Reckoning* is no different. There are characters that you know and love (and hate LOL), and there are some that you have been newly introduced to, but what else is new, right?

I feel like we're family after going through so many books with you, but let's do this anyway.

With *Reckoning*, as usual, I took a few cases and put my usual twist on them, making sure the persons would remain nameless and faceless. I did things a little differently this time, and I'm honestly worried about what you might think about everything that has happened in this installment. Hell, Dom is still a little irritated with me, but I can't do anything about that. Sometimes, things happen, and for every action, there is an equal, opposite reaction. This one hurt to pen together, trust me on that, and you'll find out why soon enough.

I have to get this part out of the way, if for no other reason than the fact that it takes a lot of people to put books together, and a lot of the times, it takes a support system to help push the artist in the direction they need to go.

As always, I couldn't have done this book without my Beloved. I haven't run out of things to say that could express how much your support and faith in my talent mean to me. This is nowhere near over with, and it should be more interesting in the future. I love you. ☺

To my mother and sister, I love you dearly. Hopefully by now, I've gotten the hang of this to the point to where you know what's coming, but I still manage to find a twist or two that even you two never saw coming. ☺

To my boss, Zane, for your continued support of my literary endeavors, I can never thank you enough for letting me roar in my own unique way. I hope to continue to give you quality heat and the passion that I have in me with each passing project.

To my editor, Charmaine, I know every so often you have those "what in the world has he done now" looks when you go through my projects. Thank you for making me look even better than I already look. You are truly a treasure to behold.

To my agent, N'Tyse, none of this professional stuff would have been possible without your help and guidance. Don't worry, He's not done with my creativity yet, so you know I've got some new stuff coming.

I'm going to end this in the usual fashion because I still have more projects to finish, burning up the pages and then some (but you're used to me by now, right?), and I know I'm missing a whole gang of folks, so just do me a favor and insert your name in this next statement:

I'd like to thank _____ for the support and love. I hope to continue to put books out that you will want to tell your friends and family about.

Thank you for reading, and God Bless you.

SPECIAL NOTE TO READERS

The grammatical errors that you might see within the dialog between the characters are not oversights. This is the type of speech and text that is used in some facets of the BDSM world. As one of my submissive friends put it, "The lowercase letters in a slave's or submissive's name are a demonstration of the hierarchical relationship. It is a reminder to the submissive that he or she is the bottom part of the hierarchy, meant to be led, and the Dominant's name is always capitalized, as He or She is the Top part, meant to lead." In keeping with the essence of the series and the essence of the BDSM community, preserving the speech was paramount. It is my hope that you, the reader, will understand and appreciate the symbolism.

PROLOGUE

"I didn't do it! I swear it wasn't me!!!"

He pleaded for his life in that moment, but mere moments ago, he shouted to the deity he prayed to as his pain-pleasure threshold was being pushed to levels never before realized. His play-partner-turned-captor waited patiently to flip the switch, realizing the time drew near to close the curtains on the scene…permanently.

Being a masochist, he didn't process the extreme pain and bloodletting as anything more than the orgasm-inducing experience he'd been looking forward to for the past month. His endorphins spiked to euphoric levels, providing the out-of-body experience he would brag about to the other masochists in the submissive male group he belonged to for at least the next upcoming months. He would be the envy of his peers, wearing more than a few badges of honor as vestiges of time well spent.

The last thing he suspected was the scene of his dreams turning into a nightmare of epic proportions.

"You're going to pay for the decision you made." The scowl on the face of his tormentor should have been enough to instill the genuine fear that washed over him, and it was in that moment that he realized the fantasy was over, but the reality was beyond any conscionable comprehension. "You took someone I loved more than anyone on this planet. I'm going to make you all pay."

The gravity of the situation weighed more than the chains that were originally used to tie and bind the so-called helpless victim. The fear of the unknown was palpable, but what had him paralyzed more than anything else was the lack of an answer to the scariest question of all: *am I going to die tonight?*

Abraham Lincoln once said, "We all owe God a debt, and the debt that all men pay is death." He stared into the eyes of the debt collector, the person who would be the one who ensured he would never see another day of his life, to never see the next sunrise.

"I didn't do anything, all I did was what I am supposed to do. I'm an assistant district attorney, dammit! She broke the law!" If he was going to go, he wasn't about to go out like a scared little bitch, pleading for his life. As much as he tried, his mind was too far gone to process the wounds on his body as a credible threat to his life. It didn't stop him from voicing his anger over the cryptic turn of events. "I made the decision based on the evidence, mother-fucker! I'll be damned if I let someone tell me I did differently!"

"You made your decision when you breached protocol to have my Domina incarcerated, and all over bullshit." The icy stare coming from his captor turned more menacing by the second.

"She didn't do anything that bitch boi didn't ask for, and you know it!"

"She raped me, too!" He blurted out the information he swore he would never tell another soul once Mistress Edge was sentenced and sent to prison. "I was not about to let her get away with it! Fuck you!"

The intensity increased once finely sharpened steel plunged into pliable flesh, leaving the victim in the position of not knowing whether to scream out in pain or ecstasy as his brain found it increasingly difficult to decipher between the two. His rational brain should have recognized the imminent threat, but the pleasure centers clouded that deduction. Even the sight of more blood than usual wasn't enough to activate the fight-or-flight mechanism.

Despite his cries, his tormentor treated them as nothing more than a dead man's final requests before he ended his life.

ᒣᒣᒣ

"Please don't kill me...please don't stop...I don't want to die!" The conflict flashed across his face as the words descended into unintelligible slurs, soon to be replaced by gurgles and the coughing of blood. His eyes conveyed the fear and confusion in his mind as he recognized the finality of his life being extinguished. He wasn't ready to go, but that choice was no longer his to make.

His killer took one look into the eyes of one of the people who had taken his Domina away from him. He remembered the frantic phone call he'd received while tending to business overseas. He remembered the fear in her tone as she'd told him she had been sentenced. Those sounds would haunt him the rest of his life.

"You're going to die, of that you can be sure." Tears flowed from his eyes as his thoughts moved to the phone call he received months later from the women's prison. The warden expressed her regrets as she informed him that his precious Domina had been killed in a cafeteria riot. He looked down at his helpless victim as he took stock of the life flowing out of the body he'd been torturing for hours. "An eye for an eye: isn't that what the 'good book' says?"

He didn't realize while he reminisced that the victim had already departed from this realm and journeyed to the next. Once aware of the expulsion, he shouted skyward in a symbolic gesture to his Domina. *He's on his way for You to torture, my Domina. More will be on the way soon.*

He stood there for a few moments as he contemplated his next move. Although they weren't far from where he wanted to stage the final scene, time worked against him. It wouldn't be perfect, but it would be enough. It was the first in a series of unfortunate events that would conclude with his final objective: taking everything from Dominic Law, including his very life.

He wouldn't rest until he dispatched everyone who had a hand in her death, but he would save Dominic for last. He wanted his new nemesis to feel what he felt when she was taken from him. Before it would be said and done, he would derive the ultimate pleasure in watching the hope drain from his eyes before he put him out of his misery.

It wouldn't bring her back to him, but it was one helluva start.

ONE

"Damn, baby, get it…take that pussy!"

Tori had her ass on full display, assuming a doggie-style position, wet pussy for me to appreciate and penetrate. It was a long-awaited reward for removing some unwanted "trash" from her front door.

Actually, I had the FBI to thank for that, but she didn't have to know all the details. I was ready, willing, and able to take all the credit, and the spoils that came with it, too.

"Is it good to you, baby?" Her body swayed provocatively, giving me a tantalizing view, fueling my aggression even more than I originally thought was possible. She felt my energy on her, pulsing through her, seemingly giving her life as she took every stroke I had to give to her.

My answer came in the form of her walls being penetrated balls deep; I felt her squirm to adjust to my girth as I slid in and out of her sex with the force of a jackhammer. She rotated her hips to get a better grip on me, squealing at the sounds of the growls escaping my lips as I inhaled the primal scent in the air.

Yeah, she'd make a good slut to use when I needed her, but I needed her for more than that; she's my all-access pass to the underground network. If this was what was needed to keep that pass current, then she was going to get worn out six ways to Sunday for as long as my body could hold out.

Her moans became more primal, begging me to fuck her harder.

She felt so slick, so wet, and yet she was so damn tight it was crazy. It was almost euphoric, until another surprise came out of nowhere.

Tori felt slight stinging sensations across her ass cheeks and her lower back as I slowed down a bit. They didn't hurt, but they were definitely noticeable, even while being fucked. She looked back for reassurance, meeting my eyes with uncertainty. The smile that greeted her calmed her down immediately as I held up a vat. "Relax, sexy, it's only wax. Now, work my dick while I drip it all over you."

"Damn, D, you know I like that freaky shit." She struggled to breathe, working her hips and trembling as each drop of wax from the vat of wax I held in my hand landed all over her cappuccino-colored skin. She kept rolling her hips as the sensation became surreal for her. "Shit, you're gonna make me come...keep doing that...shit, yeah, keep doing that. I'm gonna come."

I was near my own climax and I needed to delay it. She wasn't getting away that easily. She needed to know who was in charge here. I pulled her up close to me by the hair, this time angrily whispering in her ear, "Whose pussy is this, bitch?"

"It's yours, D, it's yours. Take it, D!!!!"

"Then come on my dick now, and you better not hold back. Make me want to fuck you again," I commanded.

"Ohhhhhhh fuck, I'm coming!!!! Oh, my God, I feel it...harder, D, please!!!" Her body tensed, and she buried her face into the rug and screamed as wave after wave swept over her with a fury she wasn't quite ready for. Tori finally collapsed on the rug, still going through the aftershocks of the orgasm that she had just experienced.

But I wasn't done with her...yet.

I was just about to dive back in as I watched her ass wiggle and gyrate in the air, begging me to take her some more, when the familiar chime that let me know my partner was calling broke through the whimpers and coos escaping from Tori's lips.

"Yes, Sir, what can I do for you?" I asked as I tried to mask the shallowness in my breathing.

"I hate bothering you when you're otherwise engaged, especially on a pseudo day off, but we got a call from Niki." Ramesses sounded business-like as usual, changing my mood in an instant. "The way she sounded, it might be something we need to take a look at."

"Give me the rundown."

"Okay, according to Niki's detectives, they were called to the scene by a convenience store owner, where the body of an un-identified black male was found dumped in the bushes behind the store." He ran through the notes he read from, giving me the suspicion that he had a longer conversation than he originally let on. "The description they have is he was wearing jeans, a black T-shirt, white socks and black leather work boots. She and Trish couldn't find any ID on him, but they are still searching the crime scene. Tire tracks and footprints can be seen in the dirt near his body."

"I don't get it, Sir; it sounds like routine homicide; why are they calling us in on this?" I inquired as I watched Tori continue to writhe and grind against her fingers, trying her best to distract me. "What's the angle?"

"Well, kid, the angle is the convenience store where the body was found is about a mile away from NEBU." Ramesses finally leveled with me. "This one's close to home this time, Dominic. I think this could be a problem that we need to handle as soon as possible. If we don't stay on top of this…I don't think I need to remind you of the consequences."

He wasn't kidding. It was close to home. It could be nothing, but it could be something, especially if the body was found so close to the compound. There could be a possibility that it was a current member, which could be bad for business if anyone found out about it.

There was only one way to find out what we were dealing with.

"I'll meet you at the scene in twenty minutes, Sir," I stated quickly. Tori was still waiting to be taken again, and if I was about to deal with a homicide, I needed my mind clear. "Better make that thirty; I have some business to finish."

TWO

"Detective Sharpe, it's been a long time, sir."

We exchanged pleasantries while standing over the body of a man who, while Ramesses and I had worked with for only a short time, was a long-time colleague of Sharpe and Niki. Quite honestly, since the case that put Kacie, aka Mistress Edge, in prison on a ten-year bid, it had been at least six months since we'd last seen him. Even with the body lying in such a contorted state, his face was unmistakable.

"Law, Mr. Alexander, it has been a long time, gentlemen." Sharpe leaned down over the body, shaking his head at the state it was left in. "I wished it were under more pleasant circumstances, though."

Despite the decrepit area, he was still well-kempt before his demise; designer jeans, a black T-shirt, white socks and black leather work boots. His hair was freshly cut, no more than two days since his last visit to the barber, and his beard was meticulously trimmed. Despite all of that, his wallet, cell phone and jewelry were taken from him, presumably to conceal his identity in any form or fashion. Tire tracks and footprints could be seen in the soft dirt near his body, and trash was strewn about near the dumpster where he was placed.

The medical examiner shook her head as she tried to hold back tears. She almost looked like she wanted to hold the victim in her arms. "He was dumped here, that is for certain."

Her body language tipped me off to a more intimate connection to the victim based on her body language, but I filed that away for a more appropriate time. I had to focus on the task at hand, but I couldn't avoid the situation altogether; she really didn't try to hide her true feelings about the deceased, so there was definitely something there that needed to be probed.

"The body hasn't been at this location for very long, either. According to the employee inside the convenience store, he heard some noises in the back area, but dismissed it as stray dogs trying to get into the scraps." Sharpe wiped his brow and flipped through this notepad. "When he came out, he thought the person was drunk and called nine-one-one to report it. It wasn't until units arrived and they checked the body that the employee realized the victim was dead."

Ramesses took a look in the direction of NEBU, the obvious question dying to get out. He did his best to word it in a way that didn't sound too much, but it was the elephant in the area, and he needed to get it out of the way. "So, if the body was dumped here, what direction could they have come from?"

The medical examiner pointed toward some bruises on the body that might have provided part of the answer. "Jason was killed by asphyxiation, but these bruises are not consistent with the homicide. You see here, near his chest? And the other bruises on his arms. What do you make of it?"

Up until that moment, no one spoke the name of the victim, but it was undeniable as to who it was. Though the bruises on his face nearly made him unrecognizable, his build and identifying tattoos of "Truth & Honor" on his right bicep were a dead giveaway as to a positive ID

One of the assistant district attorneys—and a good friend—lay dead on the concrete, a victim of one of the most heinous crimes imaginable.

Now I needed to know how the ME knew who he was when, the last time I checked, he wasn't exactly dating anyone that we knew about. Considering the discretion Jason used as a member of NEBU, it wasn't difficult to deduce that he was discreet in a lot of other aspects of his life. This could make things more complicated moving forward.

Sharpe, after glancing at us and realizing the proximity of where the body was dumped, came to the only conclusion that could have been made. "I hate to say this, Mr. Alexander, but we might need to make a stop by your compound. Considering the wounds and bruises are consistent with S&M play, we have to go where the evidence is leading us."

The ME's look was priceless. I guess the underground advertising was really working; she had no idea NEBU was nearby. That's exactly the way we wanted it to be. However, the more disturbing prospect was the suggestion that something might have happened on the grounds. The way my security team was set up, there was no way something like that could have happened without one of them knowing about it and alerting me of it, regardless of time of day.

Ramesses stepped to Sharpe for a moment, his body language resembling that of someone who was guarded with the words he was about to say. "Detective, I realize the proximity of the body to my compound is an aggravating factor, but I assure you there has been no impropriety."

Leave it to the simple legalese to introduce itself into this particular case. Without Allison here, Ramesses had to act in his own interest for the time being. That conversation would be very interesting, to say the least.

Sharpe was undeterred, as expected. "Kane, I realize you're protecting your business interests, but I must insist that we investigate further. I don't think we will find anything, but I would like to eliminate the possibility so we can figure out what prudent direction we should go in."

"I don't think so." Ramesses remained stoic. He really could be stubborn when the occasion called for it, but I wasn't sure this was one of those times. "No murder occurred on the grounds; I can promise you that."

"That may be so, sir, but respectfully speaking, I'm extending a courtesy by asking you. If you want to do this the other way, all I have to do is make a call." Sharpe took a hardened stance now, making it clear to Ramesses that we could do things a certain way, based on how Ramesses wanted to proceed. It was a fine line that I walked all the time when it came to people I had a good working relationship with. "How do you want to proceed, sir?"

Ramesses was not amused by the tone Sharpe was forced to take with him. I stood near him to get into his ear. I spoke in a tone that changed his disposition slightly. "Sir, we have to cooperate with our client, remember? No matter how close to home their investigation leads them to our other business interests."

He turned to meet my eyes, nodding at hearing his directive and acknowledging it. He straightened up for a moment, staring Sharpe down to make it clear he was still not happy with the conclusion drawn. "Sharpe, as a professional courtesy, we will open the grounds to you and the medical examiner. But I will be on the property, along with one of my council members, in the interests of being transparent…fair enough?"

"Fair enough, Mr. Alexander." Sharpe extended his hand. Ramesses returned the favor, shaking hands with him in a show of good faith. "I had hoped we could come to an agreement. It is appreciated." With that out of the way, there was another issue that needed to be handled, and a call that needed to be made also. As much as we didn't want to make the call to the assistant district attorney to alert her of the homicide of her colleague, the call had to be made. She would want to be told, rather than having it get back to her by secondhand channels.

¬¬¬

It wouldn't make this any easier, though.

"Should I do the honors, or would you like to, considering the circumstances?" Sharpe understood the delicate nature of the correspondence that needed to be delivered. "I think it might come better from you than me."

I exhaled. It probably would come better hearing from me. She'd need the moment or two to grieve and react privately before getting back into work mode. At nearly two in the morning, a familiar voice delivering bad news was not as mentally or physically jarring.

I dialed her cell phone number, moving to my truck to keep the sirens and activity from drowning out the words I needed to say to let her know a fellow officer of the court—and a close friend— had been killed.

She tried her best to mask the gravelly nature of her voice, but I didn't say anything about it. Considering the lateness of the hour, it was completely understandable for her to sound less than her sexy self. "Yes, my Master, how may i serve You?"

I fought the urge to take the conversation in the direction that her greeting threatened to pull me into. I didn't want to, but I had a responsibility to make sure she was prepared for what was coming. "Niki, as much as I would love for this call to be sensual and playful, there's something I need to disclose to the assistant DA."

I heard her shifting in her bed, assuming she was sitting up to get her bearings. "What happened, Sir? If this is work-related, why isn't Sharpe or one of my other detectives calling me right now?"

The distress in her voice weakened my resolve. No one ever wanted to be the one to have to deliver "the news" to a fellow officer, regardless of the department they work in. I was sure Sharpe didn't envy my position, but he didn't exactly volunteer to take it from me, either. "There's no other way to express this, Niki. We found your co-worker, Jason Matthews, at a location near NEBU. He's dead, baby girl."

The silence over the next few moments made it difficult for me to figure out her state of mind. As officers, we processed loss in different ways; some outward, some inward. It'd been years—nearly a decade—since we'd lost a colleague in the field. There was no way of telling how she would react to this news.

Seconds later, I got her initial response. "i'll meet You at the medical examiner's office in an hour."

THREE

"We need the cameras pulled from earlier tonight, Sigma."

I had hoped the different hoops that Detective Sharpe and the medical examiner had to jump through in order to enter NEBU would have been enough to convince them that there were no improprieties, but I had to remind myself that they were investigating a homicide. At best, this was a minor inconvenience compared to securing a bench warrant at any of the county courthouses.

"Certainly, Master Ramesses, what time frames do You need to narrow down?" Sigma was ex-military, one of the primary reasons we kept him on the graveyard surveillance team. He could spot any problems and report with nauseating detail. If the incident were significant enough, he would not hesitate to wake me in the middle of the night to alert me. Combine that with the military-styled D/s family that he belonged to, and the strict Domina he served, and he made the perfect candidate to handle anything that came down the pipeline. "I did see something a little off, more so than usual, Sir. I would have contacted You earlier, but once we figured out who accompanied him, we closed out the incident."

Ramesses raised an eyebrow. "Who was involved in the incident?"

"Mr. Matthews, Sir," Sigma answered. "It was the first time he brought anyone on a guest pass during my shift. Usually, he's gone before i sign on shift, especially on a weekday. Even the gentleman he was with was odd."

That perked Sharpe's attention. "Do you remember when they showed up?"

"Yes, sir, in fact, let me pull up the cameras." He pulled up the cameras at the front entrance, looking at his notes to determine the exact time he noticed. "Yes, here it is. The hood is what alerted me because usually the members wait until after they've gotten to the dressing area to suiting up."

That was odd, even for NEBU.

Even odder was the fact that protocol demanded facial recognition before entering the grounds.

I wasn't sure about my partner, but I was livid.

"Were you able to spot them anywhere else inside the main building or on the grounds?" Sharpe asked.

Sigma looked over at Ramesses, getting the silent nod from him to continue. He shifted to another camera where we got a bird's-eye view of the public spaces. A few moments later, Jason and the mystery man were engaged in a heavy scene.

The medical examiner gasped, tipping me to more questions I needed to ask her. The scene hadn't really unfolded yet and she reacted like a jealous lover being subjected to betrayal against her will. Sharpe cut his eyes in her direction, too. With everything that she'd presumably seen in her career, an S&M scene shouldn't have her acting like a pre-pubescent virgin.

I wasn't really worried about the intensity of the scene. After all, this place had seen its share of heavy scenes over the years that could make even the most hard-core sadist blush. My worry stemmed from noticing that the man in the mask never once removed it.

Not. One. Time.

That alone was enough to give me pause. No other identifying marks, no tattoos, no way to trace him.

Well, thankfully, almost no way to trace him. The beauty of intense scenes like that was there was always some traces of DNA that needed to be scrubbed from the scene. Saliva, skin or hair that might be on the floor; he wasn't going to get away scot-free, that was for certain.

"Sigma, has the area been sanitized yet?" I asked, checking the time on my watch. Weekday protocol mandated sanitizing all play areas by 5:00 a.m. and we were coming up on that exact time. I didn't want evidence to get washed away.

A couple of mouse clicks later, Sigma answered, "The crew is beginning the sweep now, Sir."

Ramesses chimed in. "Have them delay for two hours while Detective Sharpe gets his forensics team in to collect evidence." He looked at Sharpe, giving him a cold stare. "You can get your team in here in that time frame, yes?"

Sharpe returned his stare, pulling out his cell phone and keying in a speed dial number. "Cap, I need a forensics team to the following address…yes, sir, it regards the Matthews homicide, due to the delicate nature of the situation and the victim being an officer of the court…thank you, sir. We'll be waiting."

He shut the phone off, continuing the stare-down with Ramesses. Two Alpha males regarding each other with a mutual, grudging respect, neither one willing to give ground to the other.

If Neferterri or either of their girls were here, they'd be soaking wet right now.

"Good, now that we have that settled, what's next on the menu?" I asked, knowing full well what the procedure was, but I was acting like a retired cop—which I was—who was out of the loop.

"Stop playing, Law, you haven't been gone that long." Sharpe's irritation grew by the moment. "But since you wanna play Columbo, I need the admission records so we can see who was here tonight."

If he thought we were toying with him, he might have been on the right track if the trail hadn't led to NEBU. This hit too close to home to play jokes, but he was getting a little too comfortable with some of his requests, and sooner or later, he was gonna push too far.

"Now you're being a bit abusive, Sharpe." Ramesses played the card that I thought he would have played to suppress the surveillance cameras. "I gave you latitude with the cameras, but the records requests require a bit of righteousness on your part."

"Mr. Alexander, I realize the position you're in, but—"

"I'm afraid I'm going to insist with this aspect of the investigation." Ramesses's eyes darkened, matching the irritation Sharpe still displayed from being stonewalled. "Confidentiality is the one thing I *will not* compromise."

Sharpe rubbed his hands over his face. "I forgot you know what you're doing, too. I expected this from Law, but you gotta be kidding me?"

"Yeah, and now that you know, I'll see you in about forty-eight hours. By then, we'll have the name you need to continue your investigation."

Sharpe's facial expression gave the impression that he wanted to retort, resigning himself to the fact that he wasn't going to win this round. He walked out of the room, with the medical examiner following closely. I saw my chance to corner her, so I took it. "Excuse me, Mrs.?"

"That's Ms. Terry, detective, but you can call me Collette if you would like."

"Ms. Terry, I couldn't help noticing something while you watched the video. May I be candid?"

"Very perceptive, sir, and yes, Mr. Matthews and I were seeing each other, but we kept it discreet." She caught me off guard with the level of candor she was forthright with. I half expected to hear her deny everything and give me grief along the way. "Obviously there were other things being kept discreet from me. I feel like such an idiot."

Realizing that Sharpe wouldn't be privy to this conversation, I used the latitude to pick her brain apart, but it wasn't going to happen on the premises. "Would you like to talk over drinks, maybe coffee after you're off your shift? Maybe you can get some things off your chest?"

She stared at me, her eyes regarding my motives, assessing my appeal to her palette. "Off the record, right? This doesn't get back to my superiors or anything."

"You have my word, Ms. Terry."

"If you keep calling me Ms. Terry, I'd be less inclined to have coffee with you," Collette disclosed. "You'll make me think the mic is still hot."

"Trust me, Collette, there are a lot of things that are hot on me, but there are no mics on me." I emphasized my point by doing a mock pat-down from my shoulders to my ankles.

A smile spread across her face. "Okay, detective, I'll have coffee with you. I'm off in a few hours; I'll call you at that time."

I left her to head back to my truck, receiving a text message from Ayanna that alerted me to head back to the office for a moment or two. I needed some down time anyway, especially after the early morning activity that happened way too early, in my opinion.

If for nothing else, I needed the distraction. I had a feeling this case would be taxing on Niki, and I needed to be sharper than usual to keep her emotions as balanced as I could possibly muster. She would want justice for Jason, and Jason wouldn't have wanted her as anything less than her best.

Whoever this man was that killed Jason, I hoped he had his insurance paid up. The entire Fulton County law enforcement division would spare no expense or manpower in finding out who he was and taking him down.

If I didn't get to him first.

FOUR

"Daddy, there's someone on the line for you."

"Who is it, Ayanna?"

"She won't say, Sir. All she would tell me was that it's of the utmost importance. Should I patch her through?"

I was already on the phone, taking care of a minor issue up in the DMV with one of the compounds, Thebes, so I wasn't sure I wanted to take a blind call from someone that didn't want to identify herself to my executive assistant. My instincts told me not to entertain it until I had more information, but I couldn't take the chance. In this business, something like that could cost lives. "Patch her through, baby."

I waited for Ayanna to transfer the call, wondering who the mystery woman was on the other line, and more importantly, how she knew me. "This is Law."

"Detective Law, thank you for taking my call." The woman's voice sounded familiar, but I couldn't place her, nor could I picture her face. "I need to speak with you regarding a matter of some urgency."

"Time is money, Ms. ...?"

"Ashton. Serena Ashton."

The last name had my immediate attention. The Ashtons were one of the many prominent black families in Atlanta. Along with the usual family names that got tongues wagging in this city, if anything happened of an ominous nature that could create negative press, it was a given that they would want to have this handled as discreetly as possible.

This wasn't about to be a normal case—that much was already certain—but the thing that had me baffled was how she knew me. I could understand if she knew Ramesses, but she didn't ask for him. "You will excuse me, but you have me at a bit of a disadvantage, Ms. Ashton. It's not like we run in the same circles or anything like that, so, at the risk of sounding tremendously blunt, how do you know me?"

"No, detective, we don't, but my half-sister, however, is a different story." Serena's voice sounded disturbed, almost like she didn't want to have the rest of the conversation. "You see, she also partakes in the proclivities of the lifestyle that you and Mr. Alexander enjoy. To put it more bluntly, Mr. Law, and to use your vernacular: she's a submissive. I also know she's been a regular at the place you run; I believe it's called NEBU, right?"

"And what is your half-sister's name, Serena?" I took out a pen and pad to write some information down. I had a feeling once I worked through the NEBU membership roster, I would find her name immediately. However, the minute she stressed the half-blood relationship to the woman in question, I realized that the search in the membership database wouldn't be as easy as I thought. "For that matter, what makes you think that she runs in those circles?"

"Her name is Kendyl Ashton, and I don't think she does; I know she does." Her tone suggested that I'd insulted her intelligence, but I wasn't about to apologize for my line of questioning, either. "I found your business card while going through her things in her condo. It says you guys specialize in cases of a sensitive nature when it comes to your lifestyle, is that right?"

"Yes, that's right, Ms. Ashton." Now I really needed to know what in the world was going on. Finding my business card was not a coincidence. "So, now that you have my attention, Ms. Ashton, what do you plan to do with it? Where is your sister?"

"That's what I'm hoping you will be able to help me with, detective," she acknowledged.

"Can we meet somewhere so that I can relay that information in person?"

"My office is secure and private enough for your needs, Ms. Ashton. Can you be here within the hour?"

She hesitated for a few moments before she spoke again. "It's a little past one right now, shall we say, two thirty? I have a few things in my schedule that I need to rearrange to make this happen."

"Two thirty it is. I will see you then." I hung up the phone, turning the recorder off with the intent of working through the information later tonight. I wasn't sure if I wanted to take on this case, especially with the affluent status of the families involved. The Ashtons had a habit of burying secrets when it suited them. I remembered dealing with a case when I was on the force regarding the Ashtons that got the police chief and the mayor involved every step of the way.

I could only hope the same thing didn't happen this time around.

🔫🔫🔫

"So, shall we get to the matter at hand?"

"I see that you don't like wasting time, detective."

"Hate me or love me, I get results, Ms. Ashton. I don't like having my time wasted, to be perfectly blunt with you."

"Fair enough, Detective Law, I'll get to the point." Serena shifted in the seat in my office, trying to find a way to develop a comfort level. I had designed my office for my comfort levels, not anyone else's. Even Ayanna had been able to adjust to the unique flavor of the space. "I think my sister is in trouble. She's been missing for the past twenty-four hours."

Who was she trying to fool? I needed to know the angle, so I pressed further for details. "That's hardly a problem that requires our services. Why haven't you alerted the authorities?"

"I need this handled with a degree of discretion that, quite frankly, would be difficult for APD to handle, considering our family's standing within the community." Serena began to fidget in her seat, a tell-tale sign that she was hiding something. I continued to observe, taking notes down to freestyle over later. Something was amiss; I could feel it. "I'm scared for her, detective. She said some things that I couldn't understand, and when I went to her apartment to check on her, the place was a mess. She was normally messy to begin with, but ever since she submitted to her Dominant, she had been meticulous in her duties, including the upkeep of her condo."

I stopped scribbling when she mentioned that clue. "You said she had a Dominant, yes? Do you know, or do you remember, his name?"

Serena closed her eyes, presumably to try and access her memories of whatever conversations she'd had with her sister. "She was in service to someone; I think that's what you call it. I think his name was Kraven or some crazy name like that."

"Master Kraven?" My senses were piqued, and not in a good way. Why in the hell do these new submissives always end up finding the ones that have a sketchy past? If it wasn't the sketchy, "bad boy" Dominants, it's the newbies that thought they knew it all. Kraven was a combination of both, which was saddening, but considering who he was away from the kink community…

Serena picked up on my sudden irritation and used the opening to pry. "So, you know him? Is there any way that you could find out from him where my sister is? Don't tell me, he's a bad boy, isn't he?"

I did what I could to calm myself, but the mere mention of

Kraven was enough to get Ramesses's blood pressure up, and he rarely ever got irritated. "To answer your question, Ms. Ashton, yes, he is a bad boy, but he's harmless; trust me. He's not like your garden-variety thug on the streets, but he's nowhere near a saint, either."

"I understand, detective. What do you require to get started?"

She kept giving away mixed signals that continued to throw me off. One moment, she was uncomfortable, barely making eye contact with me, and in the next moment, she's ready to get down to business, her stare nearly piercing through me. If I didn't know any better, I'd swear she was a switch within the kink community, but there was no real way to be sure. Twenty-first century kink these days didn't require being out and about as much.

Nevertheless, something's up; there were no two ways about it.

I was already worried that she waited twenty-four hours and hadn't contacted the proper authorities to report her sister missing, so I needed to get with my girls and try to find a way to slip that under the radar to keep things above board. I needed to at least take the case, if for nothing else than to find this woman before she turned up harmed beyond recognition or worse. Missing person's cases hardly ever turned up positive, although there was a glimmer of hope if I reacted in enough time.

"Standard fees apply, a half-grand a day for surveillance; I'll be able to find out everything you need to know," I explained. A few clicks of the mouse sent the contract from the printer, and the virtual payment through Ayanna sealed the deal. "I should be able to give you an idea in the next forty-eight hours maximum. Our world is small by comparison, so it shouldn't take much to find her. I'll start with Kraven and work from there."

"Thank you, detective, and I can count on your discretion, yes?"

"You won't see anything in the public eye, unless there becomes reason to," I cautioned. "After that, all bets are off."

FIVE

"So, what was the vanilla client about?"

"I'm not sure she was completely vanilla, Sir."

I couldn't put my finger on it, but there were things about her that seemed different from the average woman that I encountered these days. Her demeanor wouldn't give her away on either edge of the paradigm, and that might have been what confused me. She wasn't submissive, but she wasn't dominant, either. One thing was for certain, she wasn't strictly vanilla; she was a bit more versed in the vernacular than she might have wanted to let on.

I observed her as she walked to her car, keeping eye contact the entire time, something that I knew a submissive didn't do, even in public where things were a bit more discreet. Now that I thought about it, she might have been what Ramesses liked to call a "French vanilla" type: not quite vanilla, but not quite fully immersed in the real-time community.

Ramesses recognized something was up, too, raising an eyebrow at the boldness of her eye contact with me. He shook his head, stroking his beard as he pondered the origin of the mysterious-but-not-so-mysterious woman. "And she specifically mentioned Kraven by name, you say?"

"I made sure to make her repeat the information, to be clear about who we were dealing with." I shook my head, trying to figure out how in the world a woman the stature of Kendyl Ashton ended up dealing with the likes of Kraven. "I know he's not your favorite person to deal with, but this time you don't have to deal with him; I do."

"Yeah, but considering the clout he has in the professional circles that I run in now, especially when it comes to dealing with NEBU, I might have to deal with him, regardless of my personal feelings." Ramesses was cool, trying to calculate the next move. I couldn't blame him for measuring his moves now. He had things to consider, and his relationship with Kraven was tenuous at best, with one wrong move meaning the difference between Kraven feeling some kind of way and trying to undermine everything we'd built at NEBU. It was his political connections that got NEBU opened as a private membership entity in the first place, a move that was questionable, but necessary.

"So, what do you want to do?" I inquired.

"I know I always say the words, 'by the book,' but this time around, I think I'm gonna let you freestyle a bit, but in order for you to do that, you're gonna have to follow my lead."

ㄱㄱㄱ

Master Kraven, away from the kink community, was a heavily connected businessman by the name of Neil Stegal. He had his hands in everything from real estate to transit, and was a member of the Metro Atlanta Chamber of Commerce. He and Ramesses had hooked up a few years ago when Ramesses wanted to take NEBU public and, for a few questionable perks, Kraven convinced the Fulton County zoning board to approve the permits to classify NEBU as a bed and breakfast.

I'd heard of politics making strange bedfellows, but this had "bad idea" written all over it. I wasn't the only one who thought so;

Neferterri made her thoughts explicitly clear before her husband squeezed the trigger on the arrangement.

Over that time, he had mildly abused his perks, bringing in some of his political friends to sample the grounds and some of the slaves, much to the chagrin of the owners of the establishment. It took a lot to upset Ramesses, though Kraven nearly had him at his breaking point. Rather than trigger the termination clause, Ramesses waged a campaign to leverage some of the influence that Kraven had in his favor, pulling the majority of those friends into his camp. Before long, the perks slowly began to fade to black, and despite his complaints to his former political connections, they fell on deaf ears, as those same friends began enjoying even better perks provided by Ramesses. Kraven never really got over the power play, and ever since, he'd been trying to find ways to regain some leverage and possibly get back into NEBU, whether Ramesses liked it or not.

Driving up to his palatial estate in Duluth out in north Gwinnett County, my senses were already tilted higher than normal. I had a feeling Kraven would be combative if he thought we were there to confront him about Kendyl's whereabouts. I resolved to let my business partner take the lead and see if this would spin into the usual game of "good cop, bad cop."

"Ramesses, Dominic, this is an unexpected visit. What can I do for you two?" Kraven opened the door, a quizzical look on his face. I kept my face expressionless to keep him from figuring out anything yet. Ramesses was as stoic as I was, not intending to tip his hand, either. Since we weren't exactly law enforcement, his fight-or-flight mechanism wouldn't need to be sensitive. "I hope it isn't anything that we need to be concerned about?"

Ramesses raised his eyebrow, trying to figure out where that question came from. "Anything that *we* need to be concerned about?"

"Yes, of course, with regard to NEBU." Kraven's smile made me uneasy. I silently wondered if someone had tipped him off to our arrival. He looked at Ramesses, trying to figure out if the information he'd dropped would get a response. "I heard about the murder the other night. I would hope there is nothing that should be of any concern."

"There's nothing that is needed to sweat about in that case, Sir," Ramesses replied. His eyes narrowed for a moment before he focused on the original purpose of our visit. "There's a submissive that has gone missing who has been attached to you. We were wondering if you had any idea of where she might be."

Before Kraven could react to the question, a woman sauntered from around the corner, slipping her hands around his waist. She was a stunning blonde, nearly six feet tall, leggy and slender, with a sex appeal that couldn't be denied despite the maturity in her eyes. "Who are these handsome gentlemen, sweetie? As delicious as they look, I would love to believe they were here for me. At least, I hope they are here for me."

I smiled slightly at her dry wit, obviously meant to mask her discomfort. Her body language gave her away, and her lack of eye contact tipped off my senses. I wasn't about to say anything to her just yet, but I had a feeling I needed to before she lawyered up. "No, we're not here for you, as beautiful as you look, Mrs. Stegal, but we needed to speak with your husband about something of a sensitive nature."

She kept her eyes on me the entire time I spoke, and I tried to figure out what exactly she was trying to do: keep my attention or figure out if I liked, and wanted, what I saw. She tried so hard to be pouty and demure that she accomplished the exact opposite. It was a bit of a turnoff, to be serious.

Kraven popped his wife's ass, causing her to jump for a minute.

He obviously was not enthused about the open flirting his wife was doing in front of him. Considering that he had a few pieces on the side, I found that quite hypocritical. "Honey, let me speak with these gentlemen for a moment, please? I promise I'll be back to put you to sleep properly."

"Okay, Big Daddy. I need to get out of these clothes anyway." She winked at Ramesses before she walked away, her heels barely touching the marble floor. "It is a shame that you weren't here for other purposes. It would have been nice to be a little sore before going in to work."

I wanted to turn to laugh for a moment, but I was here for business, not entertainment, despite his wife's apparent willingness to provide the latter. "May we come in, or do you want to do this here at the door while your neighbors wonder what two gentlemen in dark suits want with you?"

He rubbed his chin, contemplating his next move. I wasn't in the mood to figure out what was going through his mind, but I had every intention of making sure he made the right decision. I noticed a nosy neighbor peeking out of her window, and I saw my chance to step up the pressure. I began walking toward her, a smile spreading across my face, waiting for the precise moment for Kraven to realize what was about to happen to him.

"Okay, you can come in!" Kraven yelled loud enough for me to hear.

I stopped in the midst of his neatly manicured lawn, only acknowledging that I heard him. I purposely stood in place, insistent upon forcing him to repeat himself. It must have worked; I felt a hand on my shoulder and a steadier tone in my ear. "Well played, young'un, well played. Let's see if the old man can tap dance inside."

Once inside, Kraven tried his best to keep his composure, though his glare in my direction was evident. It might have had something to do with the smirk on my face. "So, gentlemen, what is this about? As I told you, I'm not exactly at a point to where I need to discuss anything lifestyle related."

I rubbed my hand over my face, realizing we would be pulling teeth to make any headway. Patience was never one of my strong suits. "Kendyl Ashton. Wanna talk now?"

Ramesses and I noticed the flicker of recognition flash in his eyes before he tried to reset his poker face. The green-eyed monster reared its ugly head with the next words out of his mouth. "What do you want with my girl? The last I remembered, you both had more than you could handle."

"Let's be more specific, shall we? Kendyl was found dead, your DNA was found on her and inside of her…do we really need to paint this picture for you?" Ramesses snapped, actually catching me off guard with his more direct approach. I was a bit curious as to why he would lie like that; we hadn't even found Kendyl yet, and he was playing this like she was already dead.

His tactic worked, though; Kraven looked like he'd been punched in the gut.

I continued to observe as he grabbed for his couch, struggling to breathe, repeating his name for her over and over. "Oh my God, my heaven. You can't be gone, you can't be."

Ramesses met my gaze, mirroring the disbelief with the theatrics on display. Call us both jaded, but nothing—and no one—was ever what they seemed. Innocent until proven guilty was not as easy as the untrained eye would believe. Besides, we couldn't function that way; we left that up to the courts.

After waiting a few more moments to allow Kraven to calm down so he could answer some questions, Ramesses took over the "good cop" role. "We're sorry for your loss, Sir. I can see from your reaction that she meant a lot to you. Do you think someone wanted to harm her?"

"Ramesses, I'm not sure...I'm still in shock right now." Kraven shook his head, leaning back into the cushions of the seating. "She had no enemies."

"Maybe *you* did, Sir," I interjected, insistent on getting a rise out of him. "Your business dealings haven't exactly been, shall we say, above board."

Kraven didn't disappoint. "I'll be damned if you presume to pin this on me! My dealings have nothing to do with what happened to her!"

"But you have to admit, Master Kraven, your submissive had no enemies, to your point. Degrees of separation led us to you, since there are no other persons to connect you to her...well, at least not yet, anyway."

Kraven's laugh smacked of mockery. "You two are ones to talk. A body was dumped outside of your doorstep to, presumably, make a point. I wonder what that point might have been."

Yeah, I kept a mental note of Kraven, definitely. He showed the classic deflection and defensive actions that a guilty man would possess. I didn't want to believe that it was that simple, but he was definitely the prime suspect in my mind. I decided to play his game for a little while longer, to see if he might need to be considered an accomplice in another investigation. "I wonder what you wonder, Sir. Would you be so kind as to regale us with your musings of what the murder has to do with NEBU?"

"You can mock me all you want, Dominic. We both know your hands aren't clean, either." Kraven's attention was squarely set on me now. "I know about your 'sterling' service record with APD and Fulton County. It's no wonder you jumped at Ramesses's offer to retire and get with him."

That revelation captured Ramesses's attention. I turned to him, subtly shaking my head to keep him from acknowledging anything or trying to give his claims any credence. I switched my focus back to Kraven, who seemed pleased with himself for the moment... until I asked one simple question. "Does your wife know about your tendencies to be down with the swirl? I mean, I'm sure you love the taste of chocolate and all, but does she know everything that you've been doing? Or have you been keeping her laced and flossed so much that she's blind and blissfully ignorant of it all?"

"It's time for you both to leave...now." Kraven deadpanned, the look of pure disgust on his face. He stood, making his way to the front door, stopping for a brief moment to turn in our direction in an attempt to silently clarify that his "request" needed to be respected and adhered to. He was startled to see how close in proximity we were to him, waiting for him to open the door so we could take our leave.

What he failed to realize was that we weren't done with him... not by a long shot.

SIX

"I believe we have matters to attend to, yes?"

True to his word, Ramesses had the admissions agent sitting in Detective Sharpe's conference room, along with her lawyer, within the forty-eight-hour deadline. The room was adjacent to his office, an added convenience and an infinitely improved atmosphere from the interrogation rooms in the basement of the building.

Sigma was extremely efficient in finding the person he needed to find, literally laying waste to anyone in his path. I was impressed; he needed to work for the firm with the quickness. Keeping my ears to the ground, I found out that a few people caught a few elbows for trying to hide her from him.

Yeah, he needed to have his role expanded, and he needed to be compensated for going above and beyond the call of duty.

Detective Sharpe shook Ramesses's hand, a satisfactory grin spreading across his face. "True to your word, Mr. Alexander, but I guess I shouldn't be surprised about that. Your word has always been solid gold."

"I appreciate that, detective, but at the risk of pushing my luck, I would like to make a request."

"I kinda figured you would, Ramesses. Shoot."

"I would like to be present in the room during the questioning. I still have interests to protect."

Sharpe's face turned to stone. "You cannot be serious right now.

You know that's not going to happen, sir. Do you have any idea the procedural risk I would be taking?"

I tried to settle both men down before they got to the point to where the words became more heated than they needed to be. "Sharpe, how about if I sit in on the interview? I'm still an LEO, and it won't sidestep any procedures or protocols that department has in place. As Ramesses has said, there are business interests that we need to protect; as security director of NEBU and the other compounds, I act as proxy in the event that Ramesses cannot, for whatever reason. This would function as one of those situations."

Sharpe began to respond, but after one look in my eyes, he realized that he wasn't going to win this battle. In the interests of discretion, he knew it would be a matter of playing the usual shell game.

For sake of anonymity, we'll refer to the young lady as dulce, short for dulce de leche, and she was as sweet and demure as her scene name suggested. Her choice of attire, however, was nowhere near as demure as she was known for. In fact, she was even more conservative than usual, and that was saying a lot: calf-length skirt, sleeveless top, two-inch block heels.

Her lawyer stroked his chin as Detective Sharpe entered into the room, his face concealing any emotion he might have been bubbling underneath. One look in my direction and that calm demeanor changed in moments. "Good afternoon, detective, I'm Mr. Peal, and I'll be representing Ms. Yates in this matter. I wish to have Mr. Law removed for this interview."

Sharpe huffed, looking at me for confirmation. I shrugged my shoulders, trying to figure out what his angle was. "Don't look at me, Sharpe. I have no idea what in the world he's getting at. I have had no dealings with him at all from a legal perspective."

"I beg to differ." Mr. Peal slowly came unraveled as he continued to stare holes in my chest. "We might not have had legal dealings, but we have had dealings before. I will not allow my client to answer questions while he is in the room."

"Well, I'd hate to have your client arrested and booked for obstruction, Mr. Peal, but Mr. Law stays, as he is a direct supervisor to Ms. Yates, and he is certified. So, which will it be; does she get booked, or does he stay so we can begin?"

I didn't want to embarrass the poor man, considering the history that we actually shared. It might have had something to do with a slight incident at Liquid one fine summer night. He was still pissed at his wife every time he thought about it, and seeing me did nothing more than serve as another reminder of that embarrassment.

Not my monkey, not my circus.

Mr. Peal scribbled some notes down, resigning himself to whatever would happen next. "Very well, Detective Sharpe, begin your interview, please."

dulce's eyes were focused on mine for a brief moment, trying her best to keep from looking like she couldn't decide whether she wanted to fear me or lust over me. She had been making some overtures toward me in an attempt to try and move up the food chain at NEBU, but to no avail. I nodded in her direction, giving the silent clue that whatever she mentioned during the interview, that she would be taken care of, as long as there wasn't anything that was against policy.

Sharpe gave a nod at me before he asked his first question. He laid the picture of the suspect in front of her, observing her nonverbal responses. "I see you recognize the suspect we believe murdered a patron of your employer's establishment. Can you tell us what his name is?"

dulce looked over at Mr. Peal, looking for a clue to answer the inquiry. After he nodded, she exhaled for a moment before she responded. "I don't know his legal name, sir, but yes, I recognize him. The scene name he gave me was Illmatic; he was a regular with Mr. Matthews whenever they wanted to engage in some private scening."

"How do you know his scene name, but you don't know his legal name?" Sharpe pressed his hands against the table top. "Isn't it policy to ensure that members are carded and cataloged before they attend any events there?"

I was impressed with the first question; he must have been talking to Niki at length about some things. I didn't worry too much about it, though, considering that the conversation would eventually lead to Sharpe trying to find out for himself if the stories and myths are true. That's how Jason eventually found himself within the confines of the compound.

dulce's face lost its color, and I realized at that moment that she'd been caught in whatever she'd been doing up until this point in time. She looked at Mr. Peal again, her eyes filling with tears. He nodded again, patting his hand on top of hers, mouthing the words, "It's okay." "It is policy, yes, sir, but...Mr. Matthews, he asked me to do him a favor, and he...well, he paid me to look the other way."

I shook my head. Ramesses was going to hit the roof when he found out about this. Hell, I wasn't entirely thrilled, either, but I had to maintain my composure to keep her from losing her cool. It would be a matter of time before the flood gates would open up and trail down her face.

Sharpe continued the onslaught, looking to pin accessory charges with each damning question. "So, you were paid to break company policy, and in turn, you wittingly allowed a potential security risk onto your employer's location."

"Detective Sharpe, your question is out of line; I will not allow you to harass my client like this." Mr. Peal spoke up, trying to slow Sharpe down. He had a point; Sharpe was going in on her a bit high and tight, but it was the same tactic that I would have used in order to press for information that I needed.

The tactic worked, though. The next words out of dulce's mouth would take everyone off guard, including her attorney. "I don't want to go to jail over this. All I did was take care of a VIP client, but I'm not stupid. If I told you I was able to get the man's information behind Mr. Matthews' back, will that keep me from getting charged?"

The whole room quieted with the quickness.

I should have known she was smarter than everyone gave her credit for. I leaned against the far wall in the room, trying to contain my grin. She picked up on the conversations that we'd had more than I thought. She would always pick my brain about certain things, asking questions that, in hindsight, culminated in today's current situation. She had an ace in the hole, and it pissed Mr. Peal off that he didn't know.

Sharpe motioned for me to leave the room with him, giving dulce and her attorney time to get whatever conversation they needed to have privately. I didn't want to be in his shoes; he had been rendered useless in the span of ten seconds.

Once we were out of earshot, Sharpe looked like he wanted to burst into laughter. "Law, you're killing me with this circus you got going on. Did you know she was gonna drop that bomb like that?"

I shrugged my shoulders, trying my best not to laugh, too. "Sharpe, I would have given you the heads-up if that were the case, trust me. I'm laughing at Peal right now; I don't think he saw that freight train coming."

"That reminds me, now that you mention it." Sharpe leaned in to keep the words from getting outside of the two of us. "What in the world happened that made him want to have you removed from the interview?"

Before I could answer that question, the sweet words of my submissive tickled my eardrums. "Would You like to answer that question, Sir, or would You like me to do the honors?"

Sharpe shook his head, giving Niki a look that caused me to chuckle. "Santiago, come on, don't tell me you had something to do with that?"

Niki shrugged, winked at me, and gave the account in one simple statement. "He should have learned not to play with the big boys, so I had to teach him a lesson."

I quickly changed the subject, trying to keep Sharpe from getting too nosey. "So, what about dulce? Is she free to go once she gives up the info?"

Niki's ears perked up. "dulce is here? Why is she being interviewed?"

"She has information that is pertinent to the case involving Jason." Sharpe figured it was best to keep from beating around the bush. Technically, I didn't see a need to keep things from her, either. "She just dropped a nugget that she might have covertly gotten the real identity of the suspect, despite efforts to the contrary."

Before either of us could stop her, Niki barged into the room and plopped down into the chair across from dulce. Her eyes narrowed as she regarded the young woman across from her. I couldn't figure out exactly what she was going to do, but whatever it was, it was going to be interesting. I knew my submissive well.

She didn't disappoint. "Let's skip the bullshit, shall we? Ms. Yates, I know you have been doing some things under the table at NEBU, and I turned a blind eye to it because it wasn't causing anyone any harm. As you're now aware, that is no longer the case. You have five minutes to give up the name of the person of interest, or I not only will make things uncomfortable for you from a legal perspective, but Ramesses and Neferterri will be very interested in your outside activities."

Mentioning those two names broke the flood gates wide open. dulce couldn't get the information out quickly enough. In fact, she reached into her purse and pulled out a folded piece of paper. "Confirmed and verified, Ms. Santiago. As I explained to Detective Sharpe, I'm not trying to go to jail for nobody. I'm not that stupid."

"Thank you for your swift cooperation, dulce." Niki walked toward the door, amused at the confused look on Sharpe's face and the smirk and nod I gave her. She turned back toward dulce before she left the room, a smile on her face now that she got what she needed. "I'll see you at the roundtable discussion this weekend, yes?"

"I wouldn't miss it for the world, Niki." dulce got up from her chair in an attempt to leave. She gave me the once-over for a few seconds, smiled to herself, and headed out the door. "Oh, and tell Natasha I said hello, too. I'm looking forward to seeing her pretty ass again soon."

SEVEN

"I'm sorry, I thought I could handle it."

Catching my submissive in such a broken state was a bittersweet moment for me. On the one hand, I was accustomed to Niki keeping it together in times like this. On the other hand, it's one thing to deal with stress, but it's quite another to deal with the stress over the loss of a colleague. Seeing her in such a vulnerable state had me at the point to where I wanted to make it all better.

This wasn't the first time we'd lost a fellow officer of the court, but it had been more than a few years since the last time. It wears on you in the aftermath. It took me more than a few months to get through the loss of my first partner—the one before Niki and I partnered up—before I could actually function normally again.

Under normal circumstances, I was wary of showing any romantic overtures while she was at work, but these weren't normal circumstances. I threw caution to the wind as I held her and consoled her. The moment her head hit my chest, she let it all go, screaming into my coat to buffer the noise.

She was able to compose herself a few moments later, immediately taking out her compact to check her makeup, ensuring the new MAC smudge-proof was still intact. It cost me a pretty penny, but as Ramesses loved to say, "Nothing is too good when it makes my girls look good."

"I still can't believe he's gone," she remarked. She looked up at me, nodding at my silent question. "I guess I should have seen this coming. He showed all the signs."

"Tell me what you observed; maybe it might help us understand and figure out who was behind his murder."

Niki left my embrace, walking behind her desk to take a seat, running through the sequence of events in her head. She nodded to herself, turning her gaze to me to begin her recount. "After that whole thing with tiger's rape, he sort of stayed to himself a bit; he still did his job, but he wasn't the same Jason I had been working with and socialized with."

"Do you think it was post-traumatic stress or depression?"

"Hard to say; his performance never dropped off. In fact, he seemed more vicious than ever, and his conviction rate jumped big time." She continued the information dump, rattling off the details in near rapid-fire motion, almost like she saw the events as they happened very recently. "But he continually turned down drinks at the bar, kept saying he had other things to do. It got to the point to where everyone else stopped asking him to go out."

"So, what changed? When we were at the station, there was another woman there—"

"Collette." Niki's expression turned to one of pity as she spoke her name. "I tried to tell that girl that Jason wasn't it, but she pegged me for a hater, trying to keep him to myself. She didn't know about you; not too many do, for obvious reasons."

The smirk on her face was met with one of my own. Most women wouldn't have been cool with keeping their dating profile on the low, but Niki was not most women. Even when we were partners, she was always coy about whom she was dating, to the point to where I even wondered which team she played for.

"The bisexuality portion of the program…I don't think she was ready for all of that. I knew he was into men, but he was convinced that not too many women would be goo with that. Hell, she was the first sistah I'd seen him with. Poor girl; she had to find out like this."

I wasn't sure if she was ready to hear the information I had to give her, but in the interests of full disclosure, it needed to be done. "I'm having coffee with her to discuss her relationship with Jason. Her reaction to everything tipped me off. She might have information that might shed a different light on things."

Niki never bat an eyelash. "I was wondering if she would hit you up. She might open up another angle all right."

I smiled at her growth over the past year. In the past, that legendary Boricua temper would have boiled to the surface in an instant, causing me to spend the next few minutes readjusting her attitude. It took a few sessions with shamise and sajira to get her under control when it came to that, but she'd really come around. Natasha wasn't as heavily invested emotionally yet, so it took her less time to adjust to her new situation.

However, the body language was not lost on me. "What do you mean, and don't think I didn't catch the sarcasm in your voice, either, Niki."

Niki blushed for a moment, realizing she'd been caught. The last time she piped up, she got an over-the-knee spanking she wouldn't forget. I had no issues bending her over her own desk and reminding her of where her place was. "Sir, forgive me, i didn't mean for my tone to slip out. It's not that i'm jealous or anything, but…You know how women are around You, my Sir."

I decided it was best to handle that small transgression once we left the confines of her locale later in the evening where ear hustlers wouldn't be able to enjoy too many "eargasms" and run tell that afterward. I switched back to the case at hand, determined to pick her brain further. "What really has me confused is why all of the secrecy? We kept him out of the loop with that rape case, and then he decides to keep it on the low anyway?"

"Look, Sir, we might be turning into 'San Francisco South,' but this office comes with a lot of pressure to fit in a box." Niki leveled with me quickly. "My new-found proclivities, his bisexuality, the powers that be would rather that information not get out to the public. Believe me, they're not in the dark, but as long as we're handling business, the rest can be forgotten."

"I understand that, but why all the cloak-and-dagger secrecy at NEBU? Everyone is under a nondisclosure agreement. The penalty is so severe that it's not even worth the money for selling the story. He knew that going in."

Niki thought about it for a moment. A moment later, she shook her head in disappointment, uttering the answer to my question with one name. "dulce."

I snapped my fingers, looking disgusted that something so simple slipped by us so easily. "Damn, you're right. She stirred up too much smoke for there not to be any other fires popping up all over the place. I'll have an audit done ASAP, but we need to be thorough."

Some things couldn't be avoided, but I also took the issues personally as the director of security. The prospect of more potential problems at NEBU was something I couldn't fathom, but my naturally skeptical nature hardly ever failed me.

Well, there was this one time, but I won't bore you with the details.

My cell phone rang; the ringtone alerted me to Natasha's call. I checked the time, noticing that it was nearly six o'clock. I silently wondered why she was calling me during her shift. Not knowing if there were other ears around Natasha, I kept the tone and language professional. "Detective Reddick, I take it you're not calling to be social."

"No, Mr. Law, I wish it was a social call." Natasha's voice was clearly in business mode; there were no two ways about it. "I was called to the scene near your office, and from the looks of it, the medical examiner is calling the death a homicide, caused by asphyxiation and a broken neck. There's also another Roman numeral on the body, sir. My partner thinks it's a copycat, wants to follow up."

"It can't be a copycat, detective, that person was incarcerated. Is it possible there's a mistake?"

"Unfortunately, it is not a mistake, sir. The numeral on the body is the number five."

Niki saw the frustration mounting on my shoulders, moving from behind her desk to try and massage the tension away. She was able to listen in on the conversation once I hit the speakerphone, chiming in to see what she could do. "Hey, girl, what's the situation?"

"Copycat, Ms. Santiago, Roman Numeral murders." Natasha made sure she stayed in business mode, despite the fact that her tone clearly changed once she heard Niki's voice. "All signs point to it, but we're trying to make sure all leads pan out."

I didn't like the inference; that case was supposed to be sealed, only a few people knew all of the details, and of those people, one was dead, and the other one, outside of the three of us, was currently working the crime scene, speaking to Natasha about the details of the homicide.

That only left one person with such intimate knowledge of that murder, and more importantly, where exactly the carvings were located.

The last time I checked, she was still at the Pulaski State Prison, under close security parameters.

I hoped I was wrong, but there was only one way to find out.

777

"Well, well, well, look at what the cat dragged in."

Making the drive down to the prison to see Simone was not the easiest decision to make, but it was a necessary one to make, no matter how much I hated it.

She was the only one who could have given up such explicit details of the murder for anyone to be able to not only copycat, but take things up a notch and continue with the last Roman numeral that ended with her.

I almost regretted my decision the moment she sat down and picked up the receiver on the other end. "I don't have time to sit here with you and play 'back down memory lane' right now. That's not what I came here for."

"You came here because you want to know if I dished out some juicy details to one of my fans about the 'Roman Numeral' murders; that's why you're here." Simone cut to the heart of the matter quickly, almost reveling in the pageantry of it all. "I gotta give you credit, Dom, you do have a flair for the dramatic. You nearly made me a celebrity in here, sexy."

My temples began to throb. *Just get the information and bounce, Law.* "Obviously you spilled the tea to make yourself look sexy, so, who did you drop the information on, huh? Let's make this easy and quick and maybe you can get back to that life sentence, okay?"

Her facial expression changed quickly. She was as cold as ice in seconds. "I ain't telling you a goddamned thing. I want you to suffer through this one, the way you made me suffer all those years. However, I might be persuaded, if—"

"If, what?" I already knew the punchline to this particular sick joke, but I had no choice but to listen to the ending, no matter how torturous it would be.

She regarded my face for a few moments, putting my patience at a true premium. She couldn't hide her smirk, like she was the Cheshire cat that swallowed the canary, taking pleasure in my lack of knowledge and her new-found power-player status in this new "puzzle." "If you come and visit me more often, each time you do, I will give you a clue to who I've unleashed into your world, and the reasons why I did it."

"No deal."

"Aw, come on, Dominic, I know you, as much as that idea might repulse you." Simone's taking pleasure in my discomfort was slowly becoming a source of pure irritation for me. She leaned back in her chair, taunting me with what she potentially had to give me. "You can't resist a good puzzle; you never could. Come on, baby, it will be like old times. It's not like I'm going anywhere, right?"

Fuck. She had me there. She literally wasn't going anywhere what-soever; she wouldn't be for the next sixty years, depending on how long she lived.

I contemplated the situation, realizing that if I played my cards right, I might be able to get her to help me put this thing to bed before someone close to me died. I couldn't have that on my con-science, not again. "All right, I'll play by your rules…for now."

"Good boy, I knew you'd come around." Simone's grin widened, putting us at a contentious impasse. "Now, about that first tidbit of information."

I wanted to back out of the deal immediately, fighting the urge to simply rely on my instincts to figure this out and be done with her for the rest of my life.

Unfortunately, she was right; I couldn't resist a good puzzle.

And this puzzle was worth the unholy alliance I'd agreed to.

EIGHT

"Show me what you have, Sigma."

We sat in my office, going through the surveillance footage from NEBU that was extracted from the night in question and from other nights when Jason patronized the compound. Ramesses wanted to see specifically what he was up to, especially when it came to our mystery guest. The hope was to establish a pattern of behavior with Jason and his play partner, and perhaps we would catch him slipping, maybe getting a facial match that we could actually use to make things easy on us.

On several occasions, Jason was observed entering the grounds with his play partner; each time, dulce was seen giving Jason a kiss on the cheek, holding him longer than usual during their embrace. I couldn't believe none of my staff caught on to that move; classic pass technique.

"My guess, gentlemen, is that this was where the money changed hands. She tried to look as business-like as she could, but it's a common move among petty criminals," Sigma explained each of the steps to the letter. "Unfortunately, she's not the only one; I swept through the footage over the past month to be sure; Mr. Matthews came at other times when dulce wasn't working, and I distinctly saw three or four C-notes pass hands of at least one more employee in that span."

Ramesses remained stone-faced, but I wasn't as hard to read. This type of breech of protocol, especially when we were solvent enough to pay everyone who worked at NEBU, was disturbing to say the least.

Ramesses finally cracked, rubbing his hands over his face, clearly frustrated with the recent course of events. "We'll deal with that after we handle the larger problem at hand. What else can we extrapolate from the guest in particular?"

"Well, he did everything possible to hide his identity; he's wearing prosthetics over his face, so Mr. Matthews must have told him about the recognition software. Sigma took his fingers and widened the screen, zooming in on the things that our guest couldn't conceal. "He did, however, forget about his tattoos, and from the looks of the ones on his forearm, you might be able to get someone who can identify the design and, more specifically, where he got the ink done."

It wasn't much to go on, but it was enough to at least get some traction. The problem with tattoos was that unless the design was unique, there could be any number of artists in the country that could have done the design.

I shot a text over to Niki and Sharpe to let them know what we'd found before we moved on to the next order of business. "I'm wondering if the play partner has anything to do with this. The thing that has me tripping is that the murder is all over the news, but no one has come forward yet. Someone has something to hide."

"I don't think it's the play partner at this point." Ramesses stroked his beard, pondering the information in front of us at the moment. "Think about it; you're play partners with someone who took great pains to conceal his identity. We do it all the time, right? Even those in the scene don't really know our actual names, Dominic. That anonymity is what shelters predator and prey alike."

"Do you think the play partner didn't know who they were deal-ing with?" I thought about his theory, and it was sound, whether I wanted to believe it or not. The only reason why people know my actual name was for a lack of theatrics on my part; I simply didn't want to have to go through all of the remembering what name to give people. "Whether he gave a false name or not, his image is out there. Someone out there knows what they're dealing with. Either they're actually innocent or they're complicit in the murder."

Ramesses shook his head, trying to figure out what our next move would be. "So, Dom, what do you think the move should be? I'm out of avenues to travel down to help you figure this out."

I thought long and hard about what we could do next, and for the life of me, I couldn't figure out what that could be. Jason was meticulous, but he couldn't have been that meticulous. Even people who covered their tracks as well as he did had a lapse somewhere. It was only a matter of where that lapse happened.

I got a call from Natasha, and from the tone of her voice, one of the answers to my questions presented itself. She was also away from her partner, too; her voice inflections gave her away. "Good afternoon, my Sir, i think i have some news that will make You smile today."

"Oh, you do? Tell Me all about it, baby girl."

"We found some evidence at Jason's apartment that might link him to the person of interest that we've had a hard time identifying, Sir. Does that please You, my Master?" Natasha's voice turned more demure by the moment, waiting for the smile in my voice to present itself. "i wanted to make sure You were kept in the loop; i know how much You want to solve this as much as we do."

"That definitely pleases Me more than you realize. you're such a good girl." I heard the giggle over the phone, grinning at the power of those two words in the psyche of a submissive. "Tell Me what the evidence is so we can follow up on the leads that it should generate."

"Well, my Sir, it seems that there were a few images on Jason's computer of him and a couple. He matches the physical description of the person of interest at NEBU; i sent the picture to Your phone, my Sir."

"Good girl. I think we'll need to reward you for your hard work, My sexy girl."

If I could have seen her blush, it would have made my day. Her voice lost its edge, and she sounded more feminine than I'd heard all day. It was intoxicating; I nearly wanted to order her to take some personal time to come to my office for a little "dick-tation." I calmed my urges as much as I could, making sure that I took the sex out of my voice as best as possible.

"You promise, my Sir? i need to balance myself; the work week has been especially hard with the cases outside of the case involving Jason. If it would please You, i would really like to be put out of my misery."

I couldn't argue with that in the slightest; I hadn't had a chance to wear either one of my girls out since we got back from Hedonism a couple of weeks ago. With the pressure and grief that Niki was going through coupled with the wantonness of Natasha needing a workout, tonight was as good a time as any to blow the roof off NEBU.

However, I was going to need some assistance, and I knew just the person to help make that happen.

"Tell your sis that we're going to NEBU for some R&R tonight. I need to work off some steam."

"Yes, Sir, consider it done."

ㄱㄱㄱ

"Lady Neferterri, it is my honor to be placed in your hands tonight."

Quiet as it was kept, both of my girls had a bit of a crush of sorts, and it involved one woman in particular. In fact, they'd admitted fantasies of being at her mercy within a play scene, and I couldn't say that I blamed them, to some degree. I could, but what would be the point? The way Neferterri was with her girls during the rare times she engaged in play scenes at NEBU were the stuff of legend. Whenever she wanted to show up and show out, people buzzed about it on FetLife and in the Facebook groups for days after.

Tonight, Niki and Natasha would bottom in a scene that would bring out the primal instincts in both of them.

The pressure of having to deal with Jason's murder was getting to Niki, and the mess I was dealing with concerning the disappearance of Kendyl Ashton had gotten more ridiculous by the day. Kraven was really at the point to where he was going to cause more trouble, I could feel it, and I needed to clear my head to get things under control. I had plans to be the second half of Niki's doubleheader, while turning Natasha over to Neferterri after I'd worked her over within an inch of her life. This particular scene would definitely get tongues wagging, that was for sure. The Lady of the House of Kemet-Ka only scened next to her husband, but considering he was in the audience with their girls at his sides, it was safe to say he wouldn't be putting in work at this event.

All eyes were on us tonight.

No pressure, though. I was only working alongside one of the more revered Dominas in Atlanta and beyond. She already had a line around the corner from the minute she stepped through the door. At first glance at Niki by her side on the center stage, and the other submissives, regardless of gender, were envious of the position she was in.

Niki was with Neferterri while Natasha stuck close to me. Both girls stripped naked as we took the cleansing wipes to the spanking benches, the bondage table and the Cross that sat center stage. The crowd migrated in our direction, wondering if they would get the chance to witness another intense experience. I ignored them as I went about my routine, following my own rhythm and cadence as we ensured the seating areas were sanitized. I did my best to get into the mindset I needed to be in to work the crowd.

The look in Neferterri's eyes as she took control of Niki gave me an inkling that I needed to be at the top of my game tonight. Luckily, I had been practicing my Florentine techniques and putting in some time with the bullwhips, too. However, the moment I saw amani bringing out the vats of alcohol, the cotton swabs and the lighter torches, I knew it was going to be a bigger spectacle than I thought.

"I'm glad the ceilings are high down here, Beloved!" Ramesses shouted as he stroked shamise and sajira. "I'd hate to have the heat and flames put a damper on the show!"

"As hot as these bitches are, they might set off the fire alarms and the sprinkler systems before I ever light up this torch!" Neferterri bellowed from the stage, eliciting whistles and cheers from the crowd. She grabbed Niki by the nape of her neck and laid her on the bondage table, restraining her wrists and ankles. "But that's not gonna stop me from setting this hot bitch on fire!"

The crowd roared, providing the energy needed to put this scene onto another level. I stood in amazement; this was a side to Neferterri that I was definitely not used to, but I smiled as I watched her work Niki over with the riding crop, popping exposed flesh from head to toe. Niki lost herself in the moment quickly, straining against her binding, wanting desperately to touch the object of her fantasies and desires, only to be violently rebuffed, much to her chagrin and the crowd's delight.

Determined to sway the crowd's attention for a moment, I cracked the bullwhip, causing a sonic boom that reverberated off the walls and silenced the crowd. It even snapped Neferterri out of her zone momentarily. I noticed a smirk spread across her face before she continued to work Niki over again, doing her best to elicit the screams she wanted to hear from her.

"Oh, y'all forgot I was here? Well, allow me to introduce myself!" I yelled as I quickly switched to my twin leather floggers, barking the command for Natasha to assume the position so I could really put her ass on display and play to the crowd before the Lady of NEBU turned the tide in her favor for good.

The force of the impact of the falls on her skin caused an immediate reaction from the crowd each time. Hearing T.I.'s "No Mediocre" playing as part of the soundtrack of the scene only seemed to fuel my aggression and rhythm. Come on, now, it's the A, baby!

The crowd was rocking now, bouncing between the all-out assault and moans coming from Natasha and the bruises and welts Neferterri continued to rain down on Niki. I stole glances at Niki, watching as her hips gyrated and grinded against the air, letting me know her libido was cranking up and purring, exactly the way I liked her.

I looked down at Natasha, watching her eyes as she silently begged me to take her *there*. I nodded, a grin on my face that was meant to excite her and scare the hell out of her at the same time.

I continued swatting everywhere I knew she would react to, observing her body as it instinctively flashed and jerked, each motion serving to arouse me and take me to the point of no return. It was only a matter of time before the crowd would be tuned out and the only thing that would matter was my pleasure and release.

Those thoughts would soon get interrupted as Neferterri's penchant for fire would render anything I did from that point forward null and void. Niki screamed like her body was ablaze inside and out as the combination of the fire and the swats of the canes that I didn't notice were in Neferterri's hands took her into the stratosphere.

Her orgasmic release sounded like she could pierce glass, if there was any nearby. Her body contorted, her thighs desperate to close to brace themselves, the rest of her trembling with ferocity as the waves surged through her. She sounded feral, yet ready to be claimed and taken. It was intoxicating to witness, and the urge to cut the scenes short and wear them out was nearly too much to bear.

Natasha's screams rivaled her sister's, the pitch being brought on by my intensity as the strokes of the floggers came down with the force of an F4 tornado. I was going to have my eruption, one way or another, even if I needed help to get her off the stage. It would be a wonderful byproduct of unleashing my more sadistic tendencies, something they'd been unintentionally bringing out of me for the better part of the past year.

"Master, Master, fuck, don't stop! Please, don't stop!" Natasha finally found her words for a moment, wincing and grinding her exposed crotch against the straddle of the bench, nearly soaking it as she felt the dam coming close to breaking. "Can Your slut come for You, please? Please, i'm begging You!"

I plunged my fingers deep, making her shudder at how wide her sex was being stretched. In the next moment, her eyes narrowed shut as she grit her teeth, her nether regions finally unleashing the tsunami it planned to release, the juices spraying out near the edge of the stage, threatening to soak the first row of onlookers, mesmerized by the sight. I continued to induce the shockwaves through her body raging from her core, causing her legs to shake and strain against the restraints, the muscle definition in her legs showing off the work she'd been putting in at the gym recently.

She looked like she was going through violent convulsions, nearly triggering the dungeon monitors to intervene. Though I was slowly slipping into my own euphoric stasis, I had the wherewithal to realize they were coming for me. I held my hands up, stopping them before they could get any closer. There was a quick stare down as they tried to rely on their senses and continued to observe Natasha's helpless state. Their immediate reaction to my block was to look in Ramesses's direction.

One look from him and they took their original positions, watching the other scenes at the other stations once they realized that there was no longer danger. Ramesses made a motion to wrap the scene up, sensing that my girls were at their thresholds where they couldn't take any more.

I ratcheted up the intensity once more, showing no mercy as I triggered a series of multiple orgasms, causing Natasha to pass out on purpose in the midst of my assault. A few of the women in the audience wouldn't stop squirming in their chairs, especially when a few caught my glare in their direction. It was interesting to witness; my reputation was starting to precede me now, and after watching those women as their eyes fixated on what I was doing to Natasha, I began to understand how Ramesses felt on a daily basis.

What a difference a year made.

A few moments later, a couple of the dungeon monitors were summoned to assist in unshackling Natasha and Niki from their areas. I cradled Natasha in my arms as amani picked Niki from the table, carrying them both off stage.

Natasha slowly came out of her unconscious state, a weak smile adorning her face. "Thank you, Master. I needed every minute of that. I hope my sis is okay, though; she sounded like she really got put through some delicious torture."

I smiled, indulging in the realization that they really didn't know what was about to come next. By the time I was done with them, they would have a problem walking in the morning.

NINE

"This is Law, I have business with Simone Lassiter."

I called in a favor to one of my former sergeants to set up the phone call at the prison instead of making the trip out to North Georgia. The way I figured it, if I absolutely had to see her face to face, it would be under dire circumstances. I didn't want it to get to that, which was the reason I wanted to set things up this way.

"Law, let's make sure we do this on a limited basis," Sarge explained before he secured the line. "The microphone is hot; whatever you say, keep it on the level. It can still be made a matter of public record if it's so ordered."

"I got you, sir." I wasn't worried about the call being recorded by the powers that be; they tried to protect against, shall we say, "audio conjugal visits," so that the inmates would not have added incentive to turn on each other, sexually speaking, of course. "She won't have time to get off like that."

A few moments of silence and a few series of clicks to let me know the line was mic'd up, and the next thing I heard was Simone's voice, sounding surprised to hear from me so soon. "I take it you're stuck in a corner of sorts; I didn't expect to hear from you for at least another day or two."

I decided on an old tact that worked on her when we were in college: instead of putting her on the defensive, trying something to play to her vanity would work to my advantage. "Well, I wanted to stay ahead of the game. You always said I was more brawn than brains, right?"

Simone giggled over the phone, a good sign for me on a lot of levels. She sighed before she got her thoughts together. "You were always good for my ego, D. Now, what can I do for you?"

"We found something at the ADA's apartment, something that links the potential suspect." I offered that information to Simone for the shock factor more than anything. I wasn't telling the complete truth, but I wasn't exactly lying through my teeth, either.

"You already know who did it? Wow. That was faster than I thought." She sounded genuinely surprised. I wasn't sure how to handle that, but it didn't take too long to figure out what she was driving at. "Usually, a couple of people are dead before the lightbulb goes off in your head."

I let that insult go in order to get her to talk some more. Self-deprecation was going to have to be the order of the day. "Well, this time, the lightbulb went off early. I guess the killer got sloppy right off the bat."

"He really wasn't too bright." Simone let that tidbit slip while she thought she was talking under her breath, but the way I had the audio enhanced for the call, I could hear the guard stationed behind her—the one monitoring her time—telling her to wrap it up. "I told her that he would fuck it up."

Her? Who was the "her" that Simone was referring to?

I tried to move the conversation in the direction of her last statement, when she had a quick argument with the guard, taking her away from the conversation. There was a quiet few moments before she returned to the phone. "Sorry about that, love. I was told that we would have more than fifteen minutes to handle this call. I'd hoped to get a taste of the sex that normally drips from your voice, but I guess that won't be happening. Damn shame, too; you always had the type of voice that made women drop their panties, even though I never wore any."

"Okay, Simone, you know that's against the rules, okay?"

She started to whine, trying to get her way since she had the upper hand. "But, D, it gets so lonely in here. These women are so damn mannish. I need a real man to set my pussy on fire. When will you come see me again?"

"This conversation is over." I deadpanned.

"Wait! Wait! You need to see about your girl! The hoe on the stroll!"

That got my attention. "What do you mean, I need to see about my girl?"

"You need to see about her ASAP, dummy! If you don't, you'll be sorry. It could be a matter of life and death!"

The phone call disconnected, and no matter how many times I tried to call back, I was stonewalled at every corner. I finally called Sarge on his cell phone to figure out what the hell happened. "Sarge, did something happen that I don't know about? She was about to give me something on the case I'm working on. She mentioned a woman that she was having a conversation with; is there any way I can find out who that person was?"

"Dom, off the record, whatever she said during that call with you triggered something that made the guard get her off the call with you." Sarge sounded like he was outside the building, away from the cameras and audio. "You may have to handle things with her in person, and I'd suggest bringing a lawyer with you when you do. You know, attorney-client privilege?"

Sarge cut the call, leaving me with a bit of a bad taste in my mouth. At least he gave me a cue on how to not have the audio engaged when I do go up there to see her for more information. I sent a text to Allison to clear her schedule in the next seventy-two hours; I had a feeling I was going to need her services, and I wasn't sure if that was a good thing or not.

One thing was for certain: Simone let on quick that she knew more about this case than she wanted me to believe.

TEN

"There's no need to be scared; it's not like I'm going to kill you or anything."

Toni wasn't exactly scared. "Apprehensive" was more the term she would use, considering the uniqueness of the situation and the size of the payment, the scenario piqued her interest more than she cared to admit.

Under normal circumstances, she would have sent one of her best girls to handle the request, but he insisted that she be the "dame du nuit," going so far as to wire a $24,000 deposit into her account without so much as batting an eyelash. That alone washed away any further objections she had about handling this client personally. The lure of this particular job giving her the next three months off was too much to turn down.

The moment she entered the immaculate Buckhead townhome, she was amazed by the physical specimen in front of her. She almost questioned why *he* would pay such an exorbitant amount to have her there. *He's too fucking sexy to be paying for it.*

She noticed the display of exotic knives and swords, listening to him explain how he had each one hand-made. Her body trembled at the thought of the ice-cold steel caressing her skin. He couldn't take his eyes off Tori's exquisite body, every curve seducing him, increasing his desire to trace and slice every inch of exposed skin at his disposal.

Moving into the kitchen to find something cold to drink, he pondered the possibilities. As he slipped an ice cube into one of the glasses, he flinched for a moment, feeling the sliver slightly rip through his flesh. It didn't cut deep enough to draw blood, but it was enough to remind him of its presence. He nearly dropped the glass as an evil smile curled across his lips. She would never suspect a thing, and he would be able to get exactly what he wanted. All the planning would pay off to complete the next phase of his plan.

It was in that moment that he had the perfect idea: a shell game of sorts, with the knives as part of the game.

One winner. One loser.

The blades he wanted to use were dull and razor-sharp to the touch. The ones that were dull he knew would not break the skin, while the ones that were sharp—if he wasn't careful—would slice the skin to such a degree that blood would be drawn. In his mind, she wouldn't know the difference, thanks to a slick trick he'd learned using a popular cream whose main ingredients were menthol and methyl salicylate. By the time she'd figured it out, it would be too late.

She was dressed in the attire he specified, the black, silk-accented dress caressing her curves in ways that did her pictures a grave injustice. Her nipples were already straining against the bra, prominently displaying the arousal he knew could only come from her pleasure in seeing how attractive he was.

Morphing into the role-play character she was to become, Tori played her part to the hilt from the jump. "My Sir, I have come as you have asked me to do. I am yours to command, as you see fit."

He never spoke another word, taking her hand and leading her to the platform bed in the guest bedroom on the main level, bending her over the rails and leaving her ample ass in the air. Taking the wrist cuffs to bind her and make sure she was completely helpless, he slipped under the bed to retrieve the knives and the cream. He growled lowly as he smeared the cream over the duller knives, watching the glow of the candlelight dancing against the face of the blades.

Tori got a glimpse of the knives in his hands, wiggling her ass to entice him to come closer, cooing and moaning as she anticipated the intense scene she was about to subject herself to. She recognized the quick-release type of cuffs he'd used, and from spending her time with Dominic at NEBU, it settled her nerves a little that she was at least playing with someone who knew what he was doing. *If he plays his cards right, I'll even throw the pussy in for free.*

He lifted her up, straining her arms against their shackles, causing her to wince in pain slightly. "Watch it, sexy; I don't mind the rough stuff, but it's gonna cost you extra."

He ignored her banter, flipping the point of the knife to trace down between her breasts, applying just enough pressure to make her think her skin was being cut open. She shuddered as the pain/pleasure threshold was being pushed to the brink and they hadn't gotten warmed up yet. She cried out, her eyes narrowing in his direction as she licked her lips, silently daring him to do it again. The icy nature of the cream left in the crevices of the knife mark made its presence known immediately, giving way to the heat that simulated the illusion that he'd drawn blood and it was trickling down her body.

He continued to rake the duller knife across her stomach, her inner thighs, applying the same pressure needed to leave the remnants of the cream inside the blade marks to give her the feeling that she was being carved and sliced apart. She teased as her arousal rose to the surface, running her tongue over her lips, purring with each slice across her skin. He slammed her against the mattress again, making her arch her back to give more attention to the fullness of her hips and the beauty of her ass.

The feel of the edges of the blade against the outer folds of her vulva was enough to send her over the edge. She didn't dare jerk from the pain; as good as the other slices against her skin felt, she didn't care too much about it; the delicate parts that belonged to her clit and inner walls were not anything she wanted to take chances with.

What she didn't realize was her play partner had made the switch that would take the scene into a sexually heightened direction... and a dangerous one, too.

"I see someone's enjoying the blades." He felt her grunt as he slipped the tip of the blade inside her walls, taking delight in her discomfort as he teased and threatened to slide it deeper inside her. "Does it frighten you to have a knife deep inside you? I know you like it; I can feel you grinding against my blade, slut."

"Ohhhhhhh fuck! Yes, Sir, I love it. I'm gonna come!" The waves wreaked havoc through her body, causing her to try to close her legs to brace for the tingles through her body. "Fuck my pussy with that fucking knife! Make me cream all over it, D!"

Her throes of orgasmic bliss were halted in an instant when he landed a stinging blow against her ass cheeks, snapping her back into the reality of her situation faster than she was prepared for. She looked up, noticing the scowl on his face. Instantly, she knew what she'd done; she'd replaced her client with Dom. "I'm sorry, I did—"

"Who the fuck told you to come, slut?" While she was relieved that he wasn't pissed about the Freudian slip, she did realize that she came out of character, a breach of the rules. His eyes darkened, giving an ominous vibe to the situation. "I should beat your ass black and blue for disobeying me!"

"No one, Sir, no one!" She couldn't stop the aftershocks from roiling through her, biting her lip to stifle the moans rising in her throat. "Please, forgive me, Sir; it won't happen again, I beg you!"

Gripping her silken mane and twisting it in his fingers, he snatched her head back, causing her to instinctively kneel atop the mattress. He accessed the quick-releases on the wrist cuffs, taking the knife lodged inside her nether regions before flipping her over and spreading her legs wide. He kneeled between them, admiring the view, the knives still in his possession.

The whole scene had played out in ways that he only imagined, each move made bringing him closer to the outcome he had in mind. It seemed too easy, so effortless, to the point to where he wasn't sure if he wanted it to end this way. He wanted more of a challenge, but he didn't want to be too ungrateful, either. The big prize would soon find itself worthy of his time and effort. He looked forward to that as he took one last look at his prey.

Yes, this would be how the game would end. He wanted her to see the end coming, and he wanted her to fight, despite the resistance being futile. He needed the adrenaline rush; the rush of her fear would fuel his aggression before he dispatched her to the next world.

He buried himself deep inside of Tori, slamming into her on the down stroke, slowly easing out of her before slamming into her again. She reached around and clawed his back, urging him, begging him to slam into her again. He obliged, but only at his pace, making sure she remembered who was in control.

Tori's frustration began to surface, no longer wanting to stay in character as they'd agreed. "You're killing me, dammit! Give me the dick! Fuck!"

He chuckled at the irony of her last statement. *Famous last words.* He couldn't believe how much fun it would be to end this at the right moment. It would be rather poetic in a sense, the way he felt.

He moved his hand to her hip, holding her down so he could keep control over how he wanted to have his way with her. She tried to protest, which only turned him on more, as she moaned loudly and dug her nails into his lower back. He groaned, grabbing her hands with his, pinning them above her head, glaring down at her, daring her to try to resist again. The evil look in his eyes didn't deter Tori one bit; she kept her stun gun under one of the pillows to reach for in case the situation turned crazy.

He slipped his fingers between their sweaty bodies, stroking her clit to change whatever thoughts that were going through her head at the moment. He didn't want her thinking that she was in imminent danger until it was too late. He noticed her catch her breath as he slammed deep, watching her eyes narrow as she tried to ignore her body's attempt to tell her that he was bigger than they originally thought. He kept her hands pinned with one of his massive paws, using the other to pull and pinch her nipples, making sure not to ignore either one, taking great delight in watching her squirm.

He thrust deeper, this time with purpose. This was the crescendo, the climax he wanted to experience before he finally completed his task. At this point, he no longer cared if DNA was found on her anymore; he *wanted* the authorities to know who did this. In fact, the knowledge that one person in particular knew what he'd done was enough to take his high to heights that he had no idea was possible. He nearly forgot that he needed to release her to grab the knife he'd saved for the final slice.

Tori was so far gone, she was completely oblivious to what was happening around her. She lost herself in the rhythm, lifting her hips off the ground to match his strokes, reaching out to him to pull him deeper so she could get off one more time. She couldn't speak; her words were reduced to a series of sighs and screams, her eyes closed as she concentrated on her pending series of deaths that she had no choice but to die, no matter how badly she willed her body to hold out until she was ready.

Unfortunately, she also wasn't ready for the blade plunging deep into her chest cavity.

Her body reacted slowly to the unexpected, and deadly, change of events, still going through the throes of orgasm as the pain/pleasure centers in her brain couldn't decipher that she was in danger. The slice across her throat was more pronounced; it had her attention, but it was too late.

She gurgled, struggling to breathe, all while he continued to pound away inside her, the dispassionate look in his eyes proving to be the last thing that she would see before the life drained from her body. The sadistic pleasure he'd gotten, complete with mixing his semen with the blood that stained the sheets, should have sated his thirst to fulfill his quest to avenge his former owner.

Instead, in his mind, it simply ignited something much more insidious.

The reckoning was not complete. His nemesis had not suffered enough.

ELEVEN

In order for me to figure out if Kraven was who I needed to focus on as a primary person of interest, I needed to find out more about him.

In the Information Age, that was as easy as performing a few simple keystrokes. Well, for normal people, anyway. In my instance, having a high GCIC clearance was beneficial on levels that the average civilian wouldn't have a clue about. It allowed me to peek a bit deeper into the things that average people couldn't see, nor should they have that ability to.

Ramesses had his sources, too, and together we were able to put together a profile to get a better and more comprehensive look at Mr. Segal. He reached out into areas I didn't know he had influence in, which was impressive—and equally disturbing. I made a mental note not to get on his bad side and try to disappear; watching him work would have scared even the most ardent conspiracy theorist.

By the time we were done with the profile, I'd almost wished we hadn't bothered in the first place.

How in the hell was a man in his late fifties able to have this type of paper trail, business and criminal, and still have the type of reputation—speckled and sketchy, of course, but it was also polarizing—that still had him recognized as a pillar of the community was beyond my understanding. I flipped through the pages like I should have been building a case on his prior crimes alone, if the statutes hadn't already run out.

As it turned out, Mr. Segal had been in trouble with the law off and on since his youth. It wasn't big-time criminalities like robbery or grand theft auto or anything like that, but it was a series of criminal mischief charges that somehow got reduced from felonies to misdemeanors, with the arrests all but wiped from the perfunctory searches that businesses usually conduct whenever they were looking at a prospective employee. However, a cross-reference of the judges in those particular cases made it disturbingly obvious as to how all of that was accomplished: his father was a State Superior Court judge in his home state of Oregon.

Back in those days, according to Ramesses's father, you could get away with a lot if you had the right connections, especially since there were no such things as computers or electronic filing systems back then. It was nothing to have paperwork somehow get misplaced or outright disappear, the proverbial shrug in response to the question of the actual whereabouts of said paperwork. That gave me pause as to what the elder Mr. Segal had covered up for his son.

Fast-forwarding to his mid-twenties, and Segal had found the kink community in northern California during the late seventies after he relocated after college, where he attended Stanford University and picked up his business degree. He managed to settle into the Oakland/San Francisco area and set up shop, trying to get a couple of businesses off the ground, using his inheritance as seed money. From a kink perspective, he'd managed to create the first of three scene aliases that he went by: Master Invictus.

He'd managed to make a name for himself, and that's not exactly a good thing. It wasn't completely a bad thing, but there was a pattern that was established that had the entire community up in arms. However, he'd managed to develop enough connections that he'd done right by to serve as his trumpeters and insulated "yes people," making him even more of a polarizing figure, both in business and in kink. He still turned into a shrewd businessman, but by the time he'd left the area, he'd had several accusations of false imprisonment and a few charges of unsavory business practices that left a few investors broke and destitute.

Needless to say, there were a few people that did what they could to find him and ruin his reputation, wherever he managed to land. In fact, there were some that nearly made it their primary task to find out where he surfaced, if for no other reason than to get the word out about the things he did in California.

While there was a gap in his kink history for about ten years until he resurfaced in Houston, his business profile had managed to expand quite a bit, branching out into real estate via flipping houses and other investments. He'd amassed a fortune thanks to those business interests, eventually settling out of court with his former business partners in the Bay area. The diligent effort managed to work after all, at least from a business perspective; kinkwise, he'd become a ghost of sorts, as no one knew who he was when he moved to Houston.

Segal might have had the last laugh, though. The settlement came with cease-and-desist defamation letters that kept them from speaking his name or discussing their connection to him to anyone. Smart move, but there was a loophole around that particular document, especially when matter of criminal justice were concerned.

He managed to keep quiet in Houston for a couple of years, going by the scene name of Master Tiernan, but his old habits in the Bay began to show themselves in time. Several women had begun to surface, each with a story of false imprisonment and being duped out of their money while investing in his newly created entertainment company. He'd leveraged this venture against his more legitimate businesses to create a sense of credibility. The entertainment company, which was supposed to be an independent film endeavor, didn't exist, and he used it to lure different women to engage in scenes that he would purportedly send to Silicon Valley for production and hopefully pitch to the larger porn studios.

Wearing out his welcome in Houston, he cut his losses and fled the city and the kink scene in the same manner as he'd done in California. He hadn't left Texas completely empty-handed, though; he now had a blushing bride, known in the local community as a switch by the name of solara. She changed her name at his direction, becoming a Domina by the name of Mistress Lohyna.

Their next destination landed them here in Atlanta, but that happened after an odyssey through the Mediterranean, including a two-year stint in Italy in an effort to have memories fade and grievances forgotten. It was interesting to have to go through InterPol to see what he'd been up to out there, but the interesting thing was that there was no hints of wrongdoings that occurred while he and Lohyna were in Italy. My guess was that he needed to make sure Lohyna was well insulated from whatever it was that he had planned for when they would return to the States.

Of course, these were simply observations, nothing more, but my observations were rarely too far off the mark. Like I said, I was damn good at what I did.

They were pretty quiet for the first few years, as Segal came back from Europe with a new outlook on things, and a new scene name: Master Kraven. Of course, old habits died hard, only this time, Kraven's desires—with his wife now in the mix—evolved into possessing multiple submissives to "share" with Lohyna, not unlike a couple whom he'd met while getting acclimated to the city. Although Lohyna was the elder in chronological years when it came to Neferterri, she'd found herself wanting to emulate the well-respected Lady of Kemet-Ka.

Before long, they were balancing their play scenes with different submissives with a new wrinkle: becoming BDSM class facilitators and presenters throughout the East Coast and the Midwest; ironically the areas of the country where they didn't incur a bad reputation.

The new strategy would have worked, except Kraven got greedy, and the pattern repeated itself in time. Before they knew it, they'd become as polarizing of figures within the Atlanta community as Kraven had been in his other two locales. There was no gray area with them; they were either hated or loved. The pressure became so intense and public opinion was so jaded that Lohyna was forced to see her husband for what his reputation was. All those years in Houston and the things he was accused of here in Atlanta, it became more and more difficult to withstand the onslaught, no matter what the excuses and explanations her husband could come up with to stem the accusations.

Between his penchant for women of color and his unscrupulous dealings that made him wealthy that she could no longer tolerate, she filed for separation about a year ago, intent on distancing herself from him and hoping to forge her own path, devoid of drama and controversy. Before long, she managed to live a reclusive lifestyle, only coming out for events and engagements that were near and dear to her. If the mood struck, she would have select people come to her home for lavish private parties to satisfy her bouts of cabin fever.

She probably would have been able to continue living like that, if it weren't for her own desires for submissives of color, regardless of gender. It would be impossible to be a hermit and still be able to attract and assume dominion over anyone.

Ramesses had found out that they had been unknowingly sharing a rather new and relatively unknown submissive who went by the name of diamante. While she went by that name publicly, Kraven changed her name to heaven; that was a name only he called her, although he was unaware of her public name, since she was extremely private about any pictures getting out into the social media platforms. It was that duality that Kendyl Ashton created that got her caught up and in her current predicament.

"I'll be damned." Ramesses shook his head as we poured over the information. If someone didn't know where to look or what to look for, they would completely miss the trail. He almost felt the need to admonish himself for being so sloppy. "I would have never done business with this nut if I'd known all of this."

"He hid his tracks pretty well, Sir." I continued to run through the paperwork, coming up on some extremely well-hidden information that I didn't think anyone—including his wife—would have ever had the thought to uncover. This new revelation was too wild to believe, and I couldn't believe that Kraven would have been so sloppy to have this come to light. "Now I see how he was able to get away with so much bullshit."

"What have you turned up?"

"Kraven isn't Kraven."

"Wait a minute, what did you just say?"

I rubbed my eyes to read the information. I had to be sure I wasn't seeing things. "Kraven changed his facial features; not once, but twice."

Ramesses paused for a moment to let that tidbit sink in. Without warning, he slammed his hand against the desktop. "So, that's how he was able to get away with everything so far. No one would have thought to dig this deep, nor would they have had the resources. As long as he didn't raise too many red flags, there would have been no need to."

"Well, there would have been no need to. He disappeared for

years before reinserting himself into a new community. Think about it; he'd amassed his fortune before he got to Houston, cashing out and paying off the business partners he had in Cali," I pointed out. "Lohyna might not even know who she was dealing with, but she wouldn't have cared anyway; as long as he didn't cross her, why would she care about some unfounded claims in her eyes?"

I understood his irritation; Ramesses was careful, bordering on the paranoid, when it came to his business dealings. Allowing a wild card like Segal could prove problematic, especially since his history had proven that he had the propensity to employ a "scorched earth" policy before relocating. "Maybe she might be willing to talk? We could flip her against her husband?"

"Perhaps we could; Lohyna has been an admirer of yours for a while now." He gave me a curious look, which had me on the defensive quickly. He read my body language, putting his hand up to try to calm me down. "She's not on that cougar kick, partner; she has taken notice of how you have been with your girls, and considering how her estranged husband acted before she left him, you might be able to get something out of her with very little trouble."

Hearing that perspective settled me down a bit. It was nice to be considered attractive when the women were your age or younger, but it was quite another when the women were knocking on sixty, even if Lohyna could put women in their thirties to shame.

"Okay, I'll check her out, see if she might have something we can use against Kraven." I tapped fists with him as I headed out the door. "She might be the angle we need to sort a few things out."

777

To say Mistress Lohyna was a free spirit was an understatement.

I had to wonder if I was in the right place when I pulled up to her house in the Virginia Highlands neighborhood. It was a polar opposite of her old life with Kraven; I suspected that was done on purpose, considering she was entitled to half of his fortune once the divorce was finalized. She almost had me convinced she was a gypsy, and once she opened the door to let me in, her stature and appearance did nothing to dispel those suspicions.

She was as exotic as her scene name suggested; there was Creole in her features, and she was in extremely great shape. It wasn't enough to change my mind, of course, but she looked damn good.

"So, Dominic, to what do I owe the unexpected pleasure?" Lohyna offered me a seat out in her back porch area. The cool breeze was a welcome feeling; considering the heat we had been dealing with the past few weeks, it felt like the proper backdrop for the type of conversation we were about to engage in. She gave me an inquisitive look, trying to figure out why I was there. "When Ramesses called to let me know You were coming, I didn't know what to think."

"My Lady, I wish this were a more pleasant visit, but I have questions to ask about—"

"My sorry excuse for a soon-to-be ex-husband." It looked like her easy-breezy attitude had nearly come to a screeching halt at the mere mention of his name. "Let Me guess, there's something else that Neal's done within the community? What did He do this time?"

"Yes, my Lady, there is something that He's been connected to, I'm afraid." There was no sugarcoating this scenario. She had to be told, if for nothing else, so she could prepare for the detectives who might come calling. "His name has come up as a person of interest in the disappearance and possible death of a submissive He was involved with. My Lady, I need to know: were You with

Him in any capacity a couple of days ago, around ten o'clock?"

Lohyna sat there a moment, trying to recall from that particular day. The more time she spent recalling that day, the more uncomfortable I became. She was trying to figure out what she wanted to conveniently forget. "I spent time with the ladies of BFD Atlanta, involved in a pretty interesting demo and discussion until sometime after eleven. Before that, I had dinner with a lovely girl who I might be taking an interest in pursuing. I think You'll like her, Dominic; she's a lot like Your girl, Niki."

I froze instantly; from the pictures that I'd seen of Kendyl, the one thing that struck me was the fact that she looked like one of Niki's younger cousins. The coincidence couldn't be more startling. It also couldn't be more heartbreaking, either; what were the chances that two Dominants of opposite gender who have no contact with each other are involved with the same submissive?

My next question felt like I was chewing on nails as I tried to form the words. "My Lady, would the girl in question go by the name of diamante?"

Her eyes widened. She had no idea I would have been able to figure out who she was talking about based on her veiled description alone. The conclusion she drew nearly knocked her out of her chair. "My God…that son of a bitch. What did He do, Dominic? What did He do?"

I wanted to say something to help calm her nerves, but the truth of the matter was that I didn't know what he did, if he did anything at all. My emotions wanted to tell her something to give her a focal point; give her something to lead me in the right direction. I couldn't do too much to give her false hope, but the look in her eyes made that task impossible. With each day, the possibility of finding Kendyl alive got slimmer. I needed something to at least give me an idea of where she might have gone.

"My Lady, I need You to listen to Me very carefully, please. I need You to try to remember if diamante told You where she was going after she left You." It was a long shot, but I had to hope that she'd developed enough of a connection that she had some influence over her. If I was lucky, she had established some sort of protocol with her, if the connection was deep enough. "Did You have a general protocol in place with her? Was she deep enough with You to have that in place?"

"As a matter of fact, Dominic, yes, we did." Her eyes lit up as she grabbed her smartphone to check the text messages and her phone tracking app. When that pulled up, I didn't know whether I wanted to balk at the concept or not. She saw my confusion and gave up a small giggle. "You should talk to Your mentor more; He's got something more invasive than this on His and Neferterri's slaves."

"I don't have a clue of what You're talking about."

"You're an awful liar, Dominic." Lohyna continued to wait for the app to come online. She gave a sigh of relief when she saw the bubble that represented Kendyl popped up. "According to the app, her phone is not too far from where My husband's house is. It looks like it's in the vicinity of Gwinnett Place Mall. Does that help at all?"

She tried to call the cell phone number, but it rang once and went directly to voicemail. I saw the frustration creep onto her face, but I was ecstatic; it was the first good lead we had on her, and it was all due to a tracking app. I almost wanted to kick myself for not thinking of it; with a techie for a partner, I was more surprised that Ramesses didn't mention that as a possible way of finding her.

"It helps more than You know, My Lady." I gave a soft kiss on her cheek as I hurried to my truck. I only hoped that she wasn't separated from her phone. It would be a positive spin on this whole missing person's situation, and considering the murder case I was working on the other end, I needed all the positivity I could get.

That hope would kick me dead square in the gut once I answered my phone. The caller ID showed a Fulton County government facility, which really put me on edge.

"Law."

"Detective, this is Collette. I'm sorry to tell you this, but we have a homicide victim out in Buckhead that I think you should see about. I found your card in her pocket. How soon can you get here?"

I checked my watch, feeling a sense of dread come over me as I felt a really eerie sense of déjà vu. "I'll be there in fifteen minutes."

TWELVE

The moment I viewed the body, I wanted to throw up.

Yeah, this was definitely déjà vu, and I wasn't sure I wanted to like the outcome of where this would head, either.

Collette did her best to explain the cause of death of the victim, but I really didn't want to hear it at the moment. I was too entranced by Tori's body laying inside of a body bag to listen to anything or anyone.

Something clicked in my mind, transposing Tori's face with Sherrie's, putting me back in the same emotional state I was in last year when she was murdered. I kneeled next to her, unsure of how to feel as the face switched from Sherrie to Tori and back again to Sherrie, seemingly putting me in a state of disarray. I was saddened that Tori was dead, but I wasn't sure that sorrow was what I was feeling, or if it was something else tormenting me. It wasn't like I was in love with Tori, but the knots I felt in the pit of my stomach could not be ignored.

Damn, how the hell did you get caught up like this?

There was no choice in the matter for me but to play this out; there was something I was missing, and I was determined to figure out what the hell it was. With Tori gone, there was no telling what else might be happening in the coming days. One thing was for sure: it was not something I was going to look forward to witnessing.

I finally blinked out of my trance long enough to hear Collette mention something that might have shone a ray of hope in this whole mess. "Wait a minute, did you say that the killer got sloppy?"

"Very sloppy, detective." She pulled a black light from her bag and walked with me to the bedroom. Once there, she moved the light over the mattress and sheets, highlighting the patterns of splattered fluids. I couldn't decipher the difference, and I wasn't about to fake it, either. She sensed my confusion and quickly put me out of my misery. "It's blood and semen, detective; the suspect made sure it was all over her even though we found used condoms near the body."

That disturbed me more than I wanted to allow. If the killer was being so careless now, then he wanted to be caught. The thing that really bugged me was the blatant manner in which he decided to show off. He might as well have scrawled a message on the walls or something, saying "I did it, I did it! Find me here!" The new game was now afoot; it wasn't a matter of whether we would catch him, but if and when we would.

I needed away from this situation before I lost my mind, and I saw the opportunity to have something pleasant to look at while I did that, while being able to focus on the other murder in this case at the same time. I looked at my watch, realizing it was coming up on shift change. "Can you meet me at Thrive near Centennial Olympic Park in a couple of hours? It will be my treat."

Collette regarded my impromptu invitation, wondering where it was coming from. "I thought you only wanted to invite me out to coffee, detective?"

"If you keep calling me 'detective,' I might have to rescind the offer and change it to the original invitation for coffee, which, if I recall correctly, you never did call me back to meet me for." I couldn't resist flirting with her; it was my defense mechanism whenever I was stressed out. "Now, can you accept an early dinner invitation and stimulating conversation—albeit with some direct questioning to help with the murder of your boyfriend—from a reasonably attractive gentleman, or would you rather have that coffee?"

A smile crept across her face as she moved closer to me so no one was within earshot of her response. "I'll see you in ninety minutes, and I'll make sure I look sexy for you. After all, if you're treating me to one of the more raved-about restaurants in the city, I think I might want to dress the part, don't you think? It is the least I can do for standing you up."

She wasn't getting away that easily, even if I did want to see what she looked like away from the job. Yes, it was the least she could do for standing me up, but that didn't exactly mean there would be anything else going on, either. "Then it's a date, Collette. I'll see you in a couple of hours."

ㄱㄱㄱ

"So, what was the deal between you and Jason? He never mentioned he was seeing anyone, but I guess now I understand why."

We were sitting inside Thrive, enjoying drinks before the entrees showed up. I was already on my second bottle of Heineken as Collette managed to enjoy her second glass of a premium Moscato bottle that I didn't realize was as expensive as it was. I was glad I had an expense account, otherwise I probably would be expecting some head or something at the end of the evening. Granted, I did invite her to the locale, but damn, I didn't expect her to take advantage.

Collette did her best to figure out exactly how she wanted to answer the question I posed. She wasn't sure which way her answer would steer things, but she eventually threw caution to the wind. "Jason and I were a 'thing' to be honest. It was only supposed to be a distraction due to my pending divorce from my husband. I thought I was able to really not develop any feelings, but you know how women are when it comes to sex. I got caught up in feelings, no matter how hard I tried."

I observed her as the entrees arrived, watching her inhale the aroma of the Cedar Plank Smoked Salmon and Zucchini plate she ordered. A brief smile popped across her face before her eyes met mine. I took my knife and made the obligatory cut into the Angus Beef Fillet to ensure that the steak was cooked to my medium-rare specifications. Satisfied with the order, I dismissed the waiter to get me another beer and another glass of wine for the lady.

"I didn't know you knew about this place," she observed, taking a bite of the meat to make sure the texture was to her liking. After a few moments of savoring the sample, she returned to her thoughts. "I thought I was the only one who knew this place existed."

"Well, I'm a bit of a foodie, truth be told, and I prefer to cook at home, but that would have been a bit inappropriate to have this type of conversation in such intimate surroundings."

The curious look she gave me had me wondering if she thought I was coming on to her. "And bringing me to a rather upscale restaurant isn't inappropriate? Don't think for a minute that I don't know what you're trying to do here. I'm not that easy, detective."

I slowed down for a minute to get things square with her. I had a feeling she needed to understand how this was supposed to go down. "Collette, I know I'm not a law enforcement officer with the department, but I am still a law enforcement officer. Do not mistake my using this atmosphere as a cover to try and wine and dine you, get you wide open so I can fuck you. You know how this was supposed to go down, since I know your connection to the deceased. Do you really want it to go down this way with Sharpe on the other side of the table instead of me?"

I watched her eyes as they darted left to right. If she arrived at the same conclusion that I arrived at before I even extended the invitation, she wouldn't be so boorish about her suspicions concerning why I was doing what I was doing. Pussy was a dime a dozen, and considering I had three at my disposal already, I didn't feel the need to be all that greedy. Not that Collette wasn't an attractive woman, but I had cases to solve, and if she could help with that, then I would not let her go until I was satisfied she could.

Collette closed her eyes and sighed, slumping her shoulders as she finally arrived at the conclusion I expected her to come to. "Okay, detective, I get it, and I'm sorry. What do you want to know?"

"Did you see anything out of the ordinary in hindsight that might give me an idea of who might have been behind this?" I didn't want to beat around the bush now. Thanks to her killing the vibe that would have made this as palatable as the cuisine we were dining on, I wasn't in the mood to be conciliatory or massage her psyche. "I know you saw something. You were at his apartment on several occasions; you must have heard something, noticed something."

Collette was taken aback by my directness, trying to shake off the change of pace and intensity as she took a sip from her wineglass. "I guess doing this subtle and smooth went out the window, huh?"

"Yes, it did. Now, if you would answer the question." I would have preferred to do things nice and easy, to let the information pour from her the way the wine was pouring from the bottle each time she emptied the glass, but that became a moot point, and she had herself to blame for that. "If you have any hard evidence that you can provide, I would greatly appreciate that, too."

Collette pulled out her smartphone, scrolled through something for a few moments, and once she found what she was looking for, she placed the phone face up on the table and slid it in my direction. "I had planned to ask him who this man was, but by the time I had the chance to get the nerve to do it, he was already dead."

I studied the picture for a few moments; it was a picture of Jason and a man I didn't recognize right off the bat. The picture was intimate, sexy. There was no question that this man was someone Jason was involved with on a carnal level. I stole a glance at Collette as she continued to enjoy her meal, noticing the discomfort she felt from even having that picture in the first place.

I was taking a risk with my next question, but I was never one to shy away from an uncomfortable situation. Besides, given her occupation, it was a necessary protective measure. "Have you been tested?"

She froze. "Why would you ask that?"

"Considering he was having sex with another person, and in this case, he was male, and there might be a chance that the sex was unprotected, it is a logical question to ask, Collette." I didn't have time to play sexual politics with her. "Answer the question."

"Yes, I have been tested. I haven't gotten the results yet; I was tested yesterday." The disgusted look on her face suggested that she was offended that she had to submit to the process to begin with. "If he was honest with me in the beginning, I wouldn't have had to be tested."

"Yeah, because cheating on your estranged husband, while having sex with your estranged husband, with the possibility of recon-ciliation, is so much better, right?" The gloves were about to come off, and she was not about to like me right about now. Jason might have been wrong for not telling her about his sexuality, but she wasn't a damn saint, either. "In fact, that's the reason why you're so dolled up right now, aren't you? It wasn't to impress me, right?"

Her eyes narrowed; she was cold and unfeeling from that mo-ment forward. "I don't know what you're talking about, and I resent the implications you're drawing, sir."

I held up her smartphone, showing the text that popped up,

dominating the picture I was studying. *I can't wait to see you, babe. Did you wear my favorite dress?*

The look on her face was priceless. "Look, it's complicated, all right? Jason was pulling away from me, and it was probably because his fruity ass was trying to be with whoever the fuck this dude is. I thought we were connecting, something I was having trouble doing with my husband. Jason listened to me, he made me feel pretty and sexy, but he knew how I felt about bisexual guys, too. That's why I'm pissed right now; he could have told me before I—"

"Before you fucked him to get back at your husband for cheating on you in the first place, right?" I slammed the door on her pity-party quickly. I paid no mind to the tears streaking down her face, especially when I'd had time to run through her information. "What other concoction are you going to come up with, Collette? There's no point in lying to me anymore; just come clean and tell me what you know or your husband will find out you're wearing your favorite dress while you're out with me."

"You're an asshole."

"And then some, and don't forget I have your phone in my possession at the current moment. I can still send the text without a moment's hesitation or second thought. I have nothing to lose, what about you?"

The gauntlet had been thrown down, and it was only a matter of time before she would blink and realize that I was not the one to fuck with. I'd done much worse, and there was not a hesitation in me to go back to doing that in order to accomplish the goal I had in mind. The feelings of a person who wanted to try to even the score on a man she obviously was still in love with was not in my circle of concern.

"Okay, stop, please!" Collette reached for her phone, snatching it from my grasp. She quickly returned the message from her husband before she composed herself long enough to begin talking again. "The guy called me from an unlisted number. I figured it might be a burner or something. He told me that the man I was fucking was not the man I thought he was, and he sent that pic and a few others that were not so lovey-dovey. I was so disgusted over the things he made Jason do, I threw up, but not until after I erased all the photos from my phone. I didn't want that filth on my phone or in my cloud."

I didn't pay that last comment any mind. As much as she didn't want it in the cloud, it was still there, and I could get Ty to pull it with ease. If anything, it might give me some other identifying markers that might tell me who this man was. I didn't want her to suffer any more than she already had, but it was obvious that she wasn't suffering as badly as she thought.

I sat there, wondering if she was going to cut the conversation short or not. After all, her husband was waiting in the wings. She had some things to do; partly making up for lost time, partly to fuck away the guilt she felt for getting caught up. She still wanted to make him pay for the wrong he'd done, but she also wanted to cover up her own wrongdoing. With the other party in no position to ever haunt her again, that would be a secret she could take to her grave.

As I observed her put her phone away and take a last sip of her wine, I noticed her eyes never met mine for more than a few minutes. It wasn't hard to figure out she was avoiding me, but it didn't matter; I got what I needed, especially since I had her cell phone number. The rest was a matter of time and patience.

"If you think I'm judging you, trust me, I'm not." I stood for a moment as she got up to leave. I made her look at me, whether she wanted to or not. "What you decide to do from here on out is your business. The only thing I care about is finding the killer."

Collette nodded, still unable to look at me. She pushed past me as her cell phone rang, no doubt her husband calling to check up on her. I sat at the table, taking the information I'd received and digested it a bit as I continued to enjoy the steak, and I pulled my smartphone to make a call.

"Ty, it's Dom. I need you to run a number and get me all the deleted pictures you can find in the past two weeks...yeah, trust me, this could be the break I was looking for."

THIRTEEN

"Wait a minute...do you care to repeat that one more time?"

The shock on my face as I listened to Niki tell me that there was a major break in the newly classified murder case of Kendyl Ashton should have put me on the floor. It probably would have, if it weren't for the irritation I felt and the sneaking suspicion that I'd been played. I wanted to punch the wall; there was no way discretion would be secured now. With the assumption that the body had been recovered, the painstaking process of speaking with the parents to inform them of their daughter's death would have to be handled.

I honestly had hoped that I—or the police detectives on the case—would have been able to locate her before having to deliver this untimely news. There was a chance that she might have been found alive, and the fact that Niki hadn't told me if the body had been discovered had me wondering how in the world this break in the case happened in the first place.

What I'd not been made aware of was that the discretion that I thought I had been operating under was sabotaged a day earlier. Kendyl's parents had gone to WSB-Channel 2 and WXIA-Channel 11 and put out a sizable reward for any information, anonymous or otherwise, for information leading to their daughter's safe recovery.

I *had* been played; this had the makings of political acceleration and the timer was ticking long before Serena came to see me. Now it was simply a matter of figuring out who the players were and what were their motivations for doing so.

Niki had become an adept player, based on the position she held. She was scant on the details; she had no choice but to be, almost to the point to where it sounded like she was trying to avoid telling me the truth. She expertly dodged every question I had in my arsenal, but she made it explicitly clear that she needed me to come down there as soon as possible to sit in on the interrogation of the suspect.

The next shock to the system was her admission that she had seen the suspect before at one of the north side munches, and that she was sure he was a lifestyle submissive. A tip had come in from the reward hotline almost within hours of the public broadcast, and he had been named in the tip as the person who was the last to see Kendyl alive. It wasn't hard to find him, either; as it turned out, he was an employee of the landscaping company that serviced the Ashton estate, among other prominent homes in the Atlanta area.

Something's not right, Law; it sounds too clean. My mind flipped; I was suspicious of everything I heard and saw from that point forward. I took the details down—such as they were—trying to keep from sounding skeptical about the whole thing. I was still convinced that Kendyl was still alive somewhere in the city, and the one burning question couldn't escape my psyche: who in the world did they have in custody?

I called Ramesses to apprise him of the situation, and he was as confused as I was. "So, they found him out of thin air or something? And he's lifestyle affiliated, too? Niki couldn't possibly be taking this seriously, could she?"

"I know My girl, Sir, and something in her voice tipped Me off that something is really off-key. She's not entirely sure, but there's only one way to find out." I couldn't escape the possibility, not for one second. Until I heard it for myself, my bullshit meter was on tilt. "I'm heading down there now. If he's lifestyle affiliated, we have interests to protect, too. We need to know who he is, who he knows, and more importantly, if he actually committed the crime."

"Yeah, we can't have anyone in the community thinking that there's a killer among us...at least until we have proof." Ramesses paused for a moment, leaving dead air between us before he made his next statement. "I'll do some more digging on the client that hired us to find her sister in the first place, see what I can turn up. Let Me know how it turns out at the precinct."

"So, tell me how you killed her, since that's what you're saying you did."

The person of interest, as I'd been told once I entered the precinct, was a man by the name of Jeremiah Taylor, but he was also a well-known submissive male who was involved with a lot of different events and people within the Atlanta community. The issue with him was that he'd managed to make a few enemies while in the business of kink-related event planning, including some who didn't take too kindly to the type of services he had some of the men who were in his employ doing. The other issue was that he had a record; it wasn't completely dirty, but it wasn't completely clean, either.

I picked the kink-related information up from Niki; I figured I'd get a more complete profile from Ramesses once I got back to the office. The other stuff I would be able to find out from the interrogation itself, but I wasn't entirely comfortable with the way things were materializing. I still felt like something was amiss, but I wouldn't be able to figure that out until I was able to witness what was taking place with the interrogation.

I sat watching as Sharpe was in the interrogation room, already sizing him up, trying to get an idea of what angle to take before he put out the first question. The unfortunate part was he took the wrong angle from the first statement he made.

"Look, I don't know who managed to snitch, but obviously whoever it was, they were in the same area that I was when Kendyl took me home that night."

Sharpe tried to not sound too skeptical, but his voice gave him away and so did his line of questioning. "Okay, so let's say I believe you for a moment, Mr. Taylor."

"Please, I hardly go by that name. Call me sirius."

"Like the satellite radio company, or like, 'are you serious right now?'" Sharpe was stoic as he asked the question, but I found it hilarious. "I'm sure you're serious; over the past year, I've been exposed to a lot within your community with the aliases and such."

sirius blinked a few moments like he was insulted. "Laugh all you want, detective, but that's how we roll. We have to maintain a sense of anonymity for obvious reasons. Everybody knows what we do is still considered somewhat illegal, so, we do what we have to do to walk in both worlds. We don't need people like *you* coming in and fucking things up for us professionally and personally because you simply don't like the way we get down."

"And speaking of professions, how did you manage to get the sweet gig at the Ashtons' estate? I'm sure it put you in close proximity to the victim, didn't it?" Sharpe was on him in a flash, cutting down his "woe is me" sob story about being persecuted. "You know, seduced her with the whole, 'come to the dark side, we have cookies,' or some shit like that?"

I took a moment to text Ramesses to give him the scene name that sirius gave up. *Let me know if that name turns up anything.*

sirius was ready to melt down, which was exactly what Sharpe wanted him to do. I guessed he wasn't too bright. "How dare you mock me? Just because you think you have me dead to rights for killing that ungrateful bitch doesn't mean you have to insult my intelligence."

"Smug son of a bitch, ain't he?" I quipped to Niki as we continued to observe behind the privacy glass. "I thought submissive males were supposed to be meek and mousy. Where did this dude come from?"

Niki stifled a giggle, shaking her head at me. "Sir, i thought after everything You'd seen in the past year or so, You would have picked up on the nuances of submissives by now. You do remember tiger, right? Do You remember anything on him that sounded like he was meek and mousy?"

She had a point, but my first impression of tiger wasn't exactly under the best of circumstances, either. We were knee-deep in the middle of a serial rape case where he was one of the victims. It took a minute for him to come back out of his shell, but from what I was told, before the incident he was one of the more outrageous personalities in the Atlanta community.

"Okay, you got Me, but this one seems a bit more self-righteous than most, don't you think? Almost like he's taking some sort of pride in what he did. That doesn't sound right at all to me." My analytical mind kicked in, moving past the lifestyle station and moving toward the supposed suspect. "I'm hoping Sharpe can get him to chat it up about how and where he did it, and where the body is now. Something doesn't feel right, Niki; My gut tells Me he had something to do with what happened to her, but he doesn't fit the profile of hard-core killer."

My attention was diverted when Sharpe asked the fifty-million-dollar question like he read my mind. "Okay, you haven't exactly told me how you killed her, though. If you don't want me to insult your intelligence, why don't you let me know what went down, and we can talk to the DA's office and get a little leniency on your time, perhaps?"

sirius paused for a minute, trying to figure out what his next move would be. He looked toward the glass, almost like he knew there was someone observing him, and he shook his head in resignation. The façade was finally fading, giving way to a man who probably hadn't done so much as picked up a few speeding tickets. "If I tell you where the body is, and I tell you how I did it, what will happen to me? Will I die? I don't want to die; it was an accident, I swear."

I wanted to feel sorry for him, but until he actually stated what happened, I couldn't be convinced that I needed to feel sorry for him. Niki stood next to me, nodding silently at my private musings, almost like she was coming to some of the same conclusions I was. Considering what had been placed out there for her consumption, she tapped on the glass to alert Sharpe to come out for a moment.

Sharpe nodded at the tapping, turning his attention back to his suspect. "Before I see what my boss wants, tell us where the body is, and she'll consider how to proceed from there."

sirius swallowed hard, realizing that his only bargaining chip might be his only chance at life. "I stashed her body in a car near the Emory Hospital emergency room last night. She was breathing when I took her there, but her pulse was weak and she had lost a lot of blood. I didn't want to be accused of killing her. You have to believe me, she's probably still there. If you hurry, you might be able to save her life."

Sharpe stood up from the table and headed out the door without a rebuttal. By the time he reached the observation area, Niki was on the phone with DeKalb County and I was chomping at the bit to get up out of there to see if what he was saying was actually true.

Sharpe had the look of a man who felt like he shouldn't be talking to sirius to begin with. He rubbed his hand over his face to try to reset his mindset before he turned to me. The question in his mind was hard and fast. "What do you think, Law? Do you think he's telling the truth?"

"I think someone put him up to this, that's what I think. He couldn't have done this; his rap sheet is muddy, but he isn't a hardened criminal." I didn't want to play the "what if" game at the current moment. I was more interested in finding Kendyl and hopefully finding her alive, one way or another. "I'm convinced I know who put him up to it, too."

Niki ended her call, looking at us with widened eyes. "The information is solid; there was a Jane Doe that was found and brought in to the emergency room last night. There was no identification on her, but I think she might be the victim we're looking for. Do you want to head up there and check it out? I can have one of the other detectives continue interrogating this witness while you figure out if that's our victim."

She didn't have to say another word.

I rushed out the door and headed out of the precinct with Sharpe, hoping that the girl they found was the victim we were looking for, when I ran into someone I didn't expect to be here under these circumstances. I wanted to remain professional, but considering I still believed he was the one who committed the crime to begin with, I didn't hide my disdain for him. "Why are you down here, Segal? Are you preparing to make a statement for the police?"

"Detective Law, fancy meeting you here. Actually, I'm here to give a positive identification of the suspect." Kraven had the nerve to look like he was really there on business. I half-looked around, wondering why he wasn't in custody or at least being escorted by officers or something. "I can't tell you how relieved I was to hear that someone had been implicated in this heinous crime."

The utter arrogance that covered his body language was enough to make me vomit. He was here to identify the suspect? I wanted to believe I was in an episode of *The Twilight Zone*, but there was no escaping this and thinking it was a bad dream. I had to deal with the reality of the situation for now.

"Wait a minute, what do you mean you're here to identify the suspect? You weren't the victim in this case; she can't make that identification, and you're not the next of kin. What bullshit are you pulling, man?"

"I was called down here to make the ID." Kraven tried to hide the smirk on his face, but Sharpe caught it, too. He put his hands up in a defensive posture, giving the impression that he wasn't there to start a fight. "You might want to stop with the harassment while you're at it, Law; I wouldn't want to have charges pressed against you, nor would I want to have an order of protection served, either."

Every fiber of my being wanted to commit the act that warranted the order of protection. I wanted to break his jaw; it would keep him from running his mouth for a few weeks and I would feel a helluva lot better for it, but it wouldn't be worth the hassle of being charged with battery and having to go to court over it. He'd play it up and make it seem like I was trying to kill him. No matter how much I felt the world would be better off for it, I had to keep my head.

"I'm absolutely convinced you had something to do with her murder, and I'm gonna be there when you're arrested and charged." I needed out of his space as soon as possible or else I was going to regret it, but not before I gave a warning that let him know that I would definitely be on his ass. "You might not want to leave town, Sir. I might have some questions for you."

"Law, listen, we don't have time for this. We have to see about that lead we have, remember?" Sharpe managed to get my attention and readjust my focus. "We can deal with Mr. Segal later."

As he pulled me toward his car, I maintained eye contact with Kraven, watching the smirk on his face and wanting to wipe it off as quickly as I could. My anger rose to the surface, but I did my best to sound as nonchalant about it as I could. "I'll be seeing you very soon, Segal. You can bet on that."

"I'm looking forward to your follow-up questions, detective." Kraven nodded as he headed inside. "Who knows, I might even be cooperative this time around and have my girlfriend serve us some tea."

I decided against hurling a snappy comeback to his last statement. I wanted to save that for when I watched Sharpe slap the cuffs on him personally and read him his rights. The way I figured it, that time was coming, and sooner than he thought.

FOURTEEN

"Yes, ma'am, we're here about the Jane Doe you're administering services to. We have reason to believe she was the victim of an assault, and we need to identify her, based on the picture that my associate has in his possession."

The nursing staff as a whole congregated around us like we were the security detail for a celebrity or something. Okay, it might have had something to do with the fact that we were dressed in suits and possessed a gait that gave the situation a heightened sense of importance, I'd admit that much. Given the seriousness of the situation, and the stress on my mind over getting this part of the case resolved as soon as humanly possible, there might have been some truth to their need to see what all the fuss was about.

I wasn't in the mood to worry about them gawking at me and Sharpe like we were the next big things on the menu; all I wanted was to make sure Kendyl was safe and sound. Nothing else mattered at that moment; the moments afterward, however, were an entirely different matter. My only problem was that Sharpe was on the hunt on more than a few levels, but as long as he didn't take up too much time getting some while handling his professional duties, I could begrudge him some time to get that done.

On the real, though, some of them had body, that's for damn sure. If I wasn't the reformed man that I was now, I'd be acting a severe fool up in here!

One of the nurses, a young and tender who looked like she was fresh out of college, was the first to speak up, once she saw the picture I gave her. "Yes, officers, she's in ICU; one of the Emory University officers discovered her body in a car last night. When we couldn't find any identification on her, we called DeKalb. I guess they got in touch with you at that point."

"Could you show us where she is, Miss?" I did my best to try not to sound too overzealous, but I didn't have time to play the small talk game right now. "She has parents that are worried sick about her, and this would be news that I know they would be grateful to hear."

She nodded, holding her hand up to acknowledge the immediacy of the moment. "My name is Kim, and yes, I'll be happy to take you wherever you need to go."

The frustrated sighs of the other nurses was comical; closed mouths never got fed, and to watch them giving the evil eye toward Kim was nothing short of shade that was born from utter desperation from the lack of choices of eligible bachelors in this city. Hell, I couldn't blame them; Sharpe probably felt like he was at a buffet in one of the Vegas hotels, and from the looks of the women, there definitely wasn't a bad choice to make among them.

I saw a couple of them try to move in our direction, looking like they were going to accompany Kim in her escorting us to where Kendyl was located, but for some odd and unknown reason, they stopped in their tracks and went about their usual duties. One look from her stopped a few of them cold; I found that curious, but I was going to leave it alone for now, unless it became relevant in the near future.

We headed up a couple of floors to the intensive care unit, and once I showed the picture to the charge nurse on the floor, she immediately recognized the picture and breathed a sigh of relief.

"God, I was hoping someone would come to claim her. The poor girl; she's been through a lot the past thirty-six hours. I can only imagine what happened to her before we brought her back to life."

Back to life? That bit of information was more than I could take. Now I really needed to see about her, at least know that she was recovering. "Can we see her, please, ma'am? This is a police matter, and we would at least like to know what her current condition is."

The nurse looked at Kim for a moment, nodding once Kim gave a nod to let her know we were legit. She sighed for a moment, trying to figure out the best way to explain the situation without getting too emotional. Once she composed herself, she began to recount what she'd witnessed over the past twenty-four hours. "Well, officer, she suffered massive blunt force trauma to her chest and head; we were able to stabilize her, but the doctors had to induce a coma so we could monitor her brain activity to make sure she wasn't in a vegetative state."

"Terri, I wasn't sure if there was any other trauma that was suffered. She was pretty bruised when we received her before we transferred her to your area." Kim helped Terri work through her flustered recount, leading her in the right direction until her emotions were better controlled.

"Yes. There was also some bruising around her vaginal area; we had a rape kit done in case she passed away during the surgery to relieve the pressure from the swelling."

The more Terri explained the situation, the angrier I became. I did my best to maintain my temper as much as I could, but I think Sharpe noticed my distress and cut her off to keep her from unwittingly poking a savage beast. "Thank you, Terri. Now, if you could point us to the room where Ms. Ashton is, we'd greatly appreciate it."

Her eyes widened when Sharpe mentioned her name, getting

excitable all over again. It was the exact reason I didn't want to mention her name; her face was unmistakable in certain celebrity circles. She fanned herself, almost like she was validated in her thoughts. "Oh, my God, I knew it was her! I remember seeing her at a benefit a couple of weeks ago. I need to call her father; he must be worried sick. I didn't want to call because I wasn't sure, but he needs to know."

Sharpe and I looked at each other, coming to the same conclusion, despite the fact that it could cause a little more stress to the situation. He approached her so she could be the only one within earshot of what he was about to say. "Terri, we would really like to be the ones to tell Mr. and Mrs. Ashton; the person who did this to her could still be on the loose and could come back to finish the job. We want to have a chance to catch them before it gets that far. Do you understand what I'm saying to you?"

From the horrified look on her face, she'd have thought her life was being threatened. She nodded, still unable to speak for a few moments before she finally found her voice. "Yes, officer, I understand. I don't want any more harm to come to her. I hope you find the person who did this to her. They need to be thrown under the jail."

We arrived at the room, careful not to disturb the other patients as we entered. As we approached the bed where she lay, I was overcome with a sense of relief that she had been found safe, though she wasn't completely out of the woods in her recovery from whatever the hell happened to her. I needed this positive spin; it did as much for my psyche as anything else could have. Sometimes you want to have the feeling that you're actually winning for a change, and that you're not always having to be on the other end of a condolence visit to the victim's family.

Sharpe must have been thinking the same thing; he dropped his hand on my shoulder to get my attention and shake me from the thoughts in my head. "Feels good to actually find one alive, doesn't it?"

"Stop reading my mind, bruh."

"Dude, you should know by now that we all still go through the struggle. Just because you're living the good life in the private sector doesn't mean you're still immune to it." Sharpe gazed down at Kendyl, shaking his head as he blinked away whatever crossed his mind in that moment. "I'm hopeful that we can figure this thing out, Law. For her sake, and our sanity."

"Speaking of sanity; any ideas of what you think might have happened to her?"

Sharpe continued to mull over the question I posed; the silence was deafening to say the least. After a few more moments, he decided to drop his theory and go from there. "Without the rape kit to see if there was actual trauma, I can't rule out that this was done by someone she knows intimately. I'm not convinced that sirius committed the actual crime, but I have a bad feeling he knows who did it and he's protecting that person by taking the fall for it."

"So, it sounds like we need to lean on him to figure out who he is connected to and figure out the connection to the victim." I was convinced we needed to leave the room; opining out loud like this with other ears listening in was not good. Thankfully, neither of us had mentioned her name while we were talking. "If we can get a solid connection, this could wrap things up quite nicely."

I hoped we would be able to wrap things up without making any more of a mess than we'd already found to begin with. At least the visit we were about to make wouldn't be as difficult as we originally anticipated. I believed they would be very relieved to know their daughter was alive, but there was no actual way to know how they would react once we told them.

There was only one way to find out.

"Oh, thank God! We were worried sick!"

The Ashtons were Civil Rights Era stalwarts, their names being mentioned in the same breath as the names of King, Abernathy, Lowery, and the like. They were, quite literally, royalty in this city, so to be able to deliver good news to them after all the strife and hardships they'd had to endure over the course of their lives was a feel-good moment for the both of us.

Mrs. Ashton was able to compose herself after tears of joy and relief flooded her face, while her husband, in true old-school reserve, managed to allow a smile to escape, a tell-tale sign that we had done well by him and his family. We were simply in awe of him to begin with; it gave us a renewed vigor to try and close this case in as little time as possible.

"You say she's at Emory University Hospital, detectives?" Mr. Ashton asked. He got a nod from Sharpe, nodding in return before he spoke again. "I don't know if I can ever thank you enough for letting us know our daughter is safe. Do you have any leads on who might have done this to her?"

"Well, that's where we were hoping you would be able to help us with, sir." I took the lead this time, leaving Sharpe to speak with Mrs. Ashton so we could compare notes once we left the house. "Do you have any idea who would want to harm your daughter? A man of your stature, and your reputation, I would shudder to think anyone would want to launch any sort of reprisal from all the work you've done over the years."

"Well, son, that's the reason why we kept both of our daughters out of the spotlight." He led me into the study, where I couldn't not notice the pictures he had on the walls of him with various leaders, regardless of ethnicity, telling a tale that, if he chose to have a memoir written or if he chose to write it himself, would be a best-seller in lightning-quick time. "Kendyl and Serena are our only two children, but they are free spirits; especially Kendyl. She always seemed to go against the grain at every possible moment, especially when she did that stint in California when she was doing some acting. She reminds me so much of her mother in that sense; Serena's mother was a polar opposite, always reserved, never really wanted to rock the boat, and she was willing to leave me to the spotlight and the criticism."

Wait a minute, did he just say his *current* wife?

I wanted to stand and head around the corner to where Sharpe and Mrs. Ashton were to get an idea of what he was referring to. Serena and Kendyl favored each other so strongly that it never occurred to me to think that they weren't born from the same couple.

At that moment, Serena walked through the door. She flinched when she saw me, which threw me off for a moment, but then it dawned on me that she probably had no idea of the latest developments.

Her father beamed, walking toward his daughter with his arms outstretched. "These fine detectives found your sister! Isn't that wonderful?!"

Serena smiled wide, tears falling from her eyes as she embraced her father. "Oh, God, that's wonderful! Where is she? Is she okay? I want to go see her now!"

"Slow down, baby, as soon as we're done talking with the detectives, we'll go and see about her." Mr. Ashton caressed his daughter's face, trying to harness her excitement and keep his own under control at the same time. He directed his attention to me, realizing that he'd almost forgotten I was there. "Forgive me, detective, I neglected to answer your question before Serena came in."

A quick glance at Serena gave me an odd vibe. She was ecstatic that her sister had been found, and maybe I was reading into it a little more than I should, but she was a bit too eager to see her sister, almost to the point to where she wanted to bolt out of the house. My paranoia was kicking in, suspecting everyone in the interests of closing the case faster. Once I realized what I was doing, I did my best to quell those urges and keep to the matter at hand. "Sir, honestly, there's no need to speak about those issues right now. The important thing is that you know where you can go and see your daughter and find out if her condition has improved."

"You're right, detective. Daddy, can we go now, please?" She sounded so girly, so teenager-girly that I was convinced it was more of a spoiled brat trying to get her way rather than my original assessment. Considering the financial status of the family, it wouldn't be too far off. She gave me another look, almost dismissive, like I'd done my job and now I could go on about my business. "Thank you, detective, I'm thrilled that things came to such a positive conclusion."

"Well, Ms. Ashton, I'm afraid that's not entirely accurate, but again, we can discuss that after you've reunited with your sister, okay?" I didn't want to tip my hand too much, but I had to let her know that nothing was over and done. Maybe her obligations to me to find her sister might have been, but there was still an assault and attempted murder to solve.

The short and intense glances we gave each other were lost on Mr. Ashton. I didn't expect him to understand the connection between us; all that mattered was that his youngest daughter was safe and sound, which should have been his solitary focus. Still, I had to wonder why she wanted to treat me like I'd grown a third eye and was no longer welcomed in her family's world.

"We are at your disposal, detective." Mr. Ashton walked to where his wife and Sharpe were talking with his daughter tucked under his arm. "I look forward to a resolution to this case also. Janice, we're going to see Kendyl; the detectives have told me where she's being cared for."

Mrs. Ashton nodded, quietly patting Sharpe's hand as she rose to her feet. "Thank you so much for the talk, Detective Sharpe, I really needed the distraction. I'm hopeful that the persons are brought to justice."

Sharpe was confused over why we were leaving so soon, but one look at Serena under Mr. Ashton's arm, and he was able to figure it out quickly. From the looks of things, he was able to get more out of her than I was out of her husband. He rose from his seat, extending his hand to Mrs. Ashton and placing his free hand on top of hers as a polite, friendly gesture. "Thank you so much for your time and conversation. We will hopefully have some good news for you in the very near future."

Once we were safely inside his car, we headed down the road, on the way back to the precinct before we went our separate ways to handle other cases. Sharpe's face was a bit contorted; he looked like whatever Mrs. Ashton told him, it was going to make things more complicated.

"Okay, what did you find out? I can tell something's up."

"Did you know Mrs. Ashton is the second Mrs. Ashton?"

"What? So, he was telling the truth about that. Hell, she's been around so long that I thought she was his only wife."

"Yeah, she married him when Serena was four years old after Serena's mother passed away. Kendyl is the second Mrs. Ashton's daughter, and Serena is her stepdaughter."

I stopped my thought process for a moment after hearing that information. I wasn't sure how I wanted to process it; the way she absolutely insisted that they go and see about her sister, it felt like genuine concern. But I also recognized that blended families could be a tough thing to grow up in. This wasn't like the Brady Bunch from back in the day; sometimes it worked, sometimes it went horribly wrong.

Sharpe kept up his intelligence dump. "Come to find out, Kendyl and Serena were fiercely competitive growing up. Serena might have been the trendsetter, but Kendyl managed to one-up her every time, up to and including when they were in college. When Kendyl graduated and headed to Cali for modeling and acting gigs, Serena took it personally, thinking she was the better-looking of the two. Do you think there might be some animosity there?"

Hearing that piece of information had me wondering whether the scope of my focus was in the wrong place, but it didn't make sense to me. Serena was the one who came to me trying to find her sister, and there's nothing that would have suggested that there was any bad blood between them, either.

"One thing is for certain, Serena hasn't done anything that would give us the inclination that she would have had anything to do with what happened to her sister. Whatever animosity they might have had, you didn't see the way she reacted when she found out her sister was alive."

"Yeah, you have a point there, but we might need to keep that on the back burner, just in case there is anything that we might have missed. You called it with the hunch on Kendyl even being alive; who knows what else we might be overlooking at the current moment?"

Sharpe was right, but I didn't want to think about it too much. The way I figured it, if I took my mind off by focusing on the other case, I would be able to come back to this one with fresher eyes and, hopefully, a way to close this thing out and be done with it. What I needed to do was get something to eat and decompress a bit; the burnout was real.

FIFTEEN

"You look like you need a drink, partner."

Man, he wasn't kidding! Having this case go from a missing person's case to a potential homicide case to an assault case in a matter of a day was worth me taking a couple of shots in the middle of the afternoon. Sure, it wasn't the best idea on the planet, but I needed to have something to settle the clutter in my mind.

I was convinced that Kraven still had something to do with her disappearance, and the minute I placed my focus back on that case, I was going to make sure that was the case. He'd been too damned smug and cavalier about it; the other things he got away with in those other cities might have had something to do with it.

Fuck that! I was going to nail him to the wall!

I headed over to the bar, grabbing one of the Scotch bottles and a few ice cubes, pouring a shot and downing it before it was over the ice cubes more than a few seconds. Ramesses sat there, observing my actions to figure out the best way to approach the conversation. "From the looks of you inhaling the good shit, I take it things took an unexpected turn."

"Kraven met me at the precinct, acting like he was a concerned party to the assault."

"I thought it was a murder case?"

"Yeah, until the person that supposedly confessed to the crime changed his story in the middle of the interrogation and said he thought she was dead, and told us where to find her." I still had to wrap my mind around that concept. My skeptical brain tried to figure out whether it was money or sex that motivated him to take the hit. "She's in an induced coma at Emory University Hospital now, and we're hoping she'll wake up and at least give us an idea of who did this to her."

"Well, hopefully you will get the chance to find that out before she does wake up. The last thing we want is for this to drag out too long. Can you imagine the craziness that would ensue if they found out about her?"

Ramesses heard his office phone ringing as we were catching up. His face showed concern as it looked like he couldn't recognize the number. With Taliah gone to a late lunch with Ayanna, the phones transferred in to the offices for us to take them directly. He debated answering it, but decided to go ahead and find out who the unknown caller might be, putting it on speaker so we could both listen in on the call.

Big mistake. "Kane Alexander, how may I assist you?"

"You can start by getting your business partner off the heaven investigation." The voice on the phone was distorted, a dead give-away that he or she was using a voice changer. "I don't think it would be in your best interest for you to pursue this any further."

Ramesses wasn't amused, but he never dealt with anything un-prepared. The skip tracing software was already activated, as it normally was whenever he took a call. Still, the call was a nuisance, and I could see the irritation rising to the surface. "And what would you know about my best interest, huh? I'm pretty sure that you know who you're dealing with, yes?"

"Yes, we know who we're dealing with: a rookie investigator and his over-the-hill, washed-up partner." The person continued to talk, the ego moment getting the best of him the entire time. "Right now, I don't think you're in a position to really say too much more, seeing as we can cancel you any time we want to, should the occasion call for it."

I'd already triangulated the area where the call was coming from, and I made sure to keep the signal live once this idiot got off the phone so we could find out exactly where he was, wherever he decided to go. Did I forget to mention that my partner was a techie, with all the latest gadgets at our disposal?

I motioned for Ramesses to keep him talking, if for nothing else but on general principle, so I could get a stronger lock on the burner that he'd planned to throw away. From where the signal was located, it was an easy mark as to where they would go once they were off the phone. I hated predictable losers who thought they got the drop on people; it never worked out for them.

I guess this one was going to find out the hard way.

"Okay, let me guess…if I don't have my partner get off the case, what will you do again?"

"Mr. Alexander, you're not taking this seriously. I'd suggest you do; the last thing we'd want to do is soil those pretty bitches of yours. Or maybe we'll see about your Beloved; isn't that what you call her, right? Maybe then you might understand the seriousness of the situation, huh?"

Ramesses flinched for a minute, and there was no way to avoid the inevitable. Dude went over the line, and I didn't know if he meant to do it, or if he was really that damn stupid to not realize he would be waking a sleeping giant? Why did they always play the "we'll hurt your family/close friends" card when they were backed into a corner? It was obvious that he wasn't aware of who he was dealing with, or the persons he had at his disposal.

Ramesses almost lost his cool for a few seconds, but he cleared his throat, and readjusted his voice to the same "devil may care" attitude he'd possessed earlier in the call. He sounded ice-cold and calculating the moment he got a moment to speak again. "Okay, I'm going to tell you how this is going to go down; when I find you—and I will find you—you're going to beg me to forgive you for threatening my family. You won't get a whiff of the perfume that my girls are wearing. Walk away now, and my face won't be the last thing you see on this earth before you leave it."

The chuckle over the phone only enraged him further. "I'd love to see you try to find me. Good luck with that."

The line went dead, and Ramesses slammed the receiver onto its base, nearly cracking the phone beyond repair. He immediately put up his hands and covered his face, chanting something I couldn't make out. It was easy to figure that he was talking himself into calming down, trying to not become the old hotheaded version of himself that shot first and asked questions later.

I tried to figure how best to approach him, finding a bit of a cruel twist of fate. The endgame was simple, too; there was only one call to make, and I wanted to give the pleasure of making that call to one very irritated business partner. "Ghost Squad?"

"You read My mind, but I have to see about something first, to confirm My suspicions."

"There's nothing to confirm, Sir; that was one of Kraven's heavies, and You know it." Sometimes, his analytical nature worked my nerves. By now, I'd be rolling with J-Roc, snatching him up by the neck and razing him, making sure he knew he was being beaten within an inch of his life. "Make the call so Me and the boys can erase this fool and send a message to Kraven about trying to be a gangster."

"I don't think you're feeling me on this one, Dom." He seemed hell-bent on figuring this out. Ever the chess player, he absolutely had to see things two or three moves ahead. "Something's not right; he was talking entirely too long, trying to bait me, get me riled up."

"Well, he did a damn good job of that; now make the call, Sir." I was nearly incensed that he was being so calm about things. That seemed to be the difference between him and me, at least in the here and now; the old Kane would have already strapped up and beat me out the door, blasting through anyone that even breathed in his direction until he got to his intended target. "We don't have time for this 'what if' game You're playing right now."

I picked up my cell phone and dialed J-Roc's number. Ramesses narrowed his eyes as he stared at me, trying to figure out why I would make the move before he gave the go-ahead. A few seconds later, he leaned forward, tapping his fingers on the desktop. "Put it on speaker."

He picked up on the second ring. "D, what's poppin'?"

"I need the boys; V12, 30-30, Illmatic, I need them all."

"Who's the idiot, and what did he do?"

"He threatened damage to the Lambo, the Ferrari and the Maserati." Those were the code names for Neferterri, shamise and sajira. Thank God that fool didn't say anything about their daughters; half of Atlanta would be in flames right now. "I have a feeling there's gonna be some others on the scene, but you know the drill: extract the target for interrogation, the rest can be sorted out by the proper authorities."

"Say no more, D. We'll meet you at the usual spot so we can go handle this."

"That's a negative, J-Roc." Ramesses cut in, glaring at me like he'd let this go far enough. "You and the squad can handle this without Dom. Bring the bitch to me, personally, so I can take care of him. Do it quietly, and there's an extra quarter in it for you."

I hoped this dude had his life insurance paid up or something;

for Ramesses to talk extra dollars on top of the usual fee, I guessed it was more personal than I'd originally let on.

J-Roc didn't flinch. "You know we'd do it for free, boss, but you take care of us; that's why we continue to fuck with you. Consider it done, and on the whisper-quiet tip. One."

Once that call was done, Ramesses made another call, one that I didn't see coming. Once I heard his voice, it gave new meaning to the phrase, "shit just got real." "Sigma, it's Ramesses. I need you to meet Me in the Cage in about three hours. I need your specialized interrogation skills; I have some information that needs to be extracted, and I expect things to get messy."

"Sir, i'm at Your disposal. i'll be there." *Click.*

Now, this was the Kane I was waiting to see! I walked over to him and tapped fists, realizing that I had some time to take care of something before I came back to witness the showcase. "I'll see You in three hours, I need to squeeze our former client to find out what she knows. There's an angle there, and I've got to find out what it is."

SIXTEEN

"Come in, Sir. I was wondering when You would be stopping by to see me."

As I stepped through the door into Serena's condo, I couldn't help wondering about the strange nature of her comment. Considering she was related to the victim, and the fact that she was the one who contracted me in the first place, she sure wasn't acting like she should be. Well, it might have been the way I thought she should be acting. Usually, it was a surprise to see someone involved with law enforcement come calling, and this wasn't exactly a social call.

The way she was dressed, however, and the manner in which she addressed me, that was definitely something that I couldn't ignore. She wasn't naked or anything, but the sarong she wore left very little to the imagination, showing off her lithe and tight body, with the assumption that it was to get my attention.

It got my attention all right, but it might not have been the attention that she thought she was getting from me.

"May I ask why you addressed Me as Sir, as opposed to detective when you opened the door?"

The confused look on her face suggested that I had her at some sort of disadvantage. She gave a slight smile as her eyes lowered and her body language resembled that of the way Natasha normally acted when she forgot that she wasn't on the streets at work. "Forgive me, Sir, i didn't mean to overstep. i was speaking to my Sir, and i guess i'm still in that mindset. i can't help myself, considering You're in my presence, i just seem to find myself compelled to be my authentic self around You."

I was more curious about the Dominant she was referring to before my arrival now.

When she first approached me with the job of finding her sister, she gave me no indication that she was in deeper than what she was showing right now. I had to remind myself that not everyone was out and proud and public, and that not everyone could afford to be so. After all, she was the daughter of a legend, as was her sister; I was certain all of her moves had to be made with the idea that eyes were always watching. For what it was worth, her Dominant could very well be in the same boat.

Once I got out of my head about her ulterior motives, there was the wantonness that she showcased that was proving difficult to have a conversation with her. It was obvious that she felt we didn't need to discuss any business, but that was exactly what I was there for, and quite frankly, I wasn't in the mood to be seduced.

I kept things on the level, the tone remaining business-like, whether she liked it or not. "How did you and your sister come into contact with the local BDSM community?"

Serena pouted, realizing that her wiles weren't having their desired effect. "You really are loyal to Your submissives, aren't You? Your reputation precedes You, Sir. To answer Your question, i found the community sometime around five years ago; i introduced my sister to it a little over a year ago."

That was interesting. How was she able to function and Ramesses nor any of the other longtime kinksters were unable to cross paths with her? "And you've been a private player the entire time?"

"Well, obviously i have to, as did Kendyl. Why else did You think

I wanted You to find her without arousing the interests of the media?" Serena answered, leading me into her living room. She invited me to sit down as she made herself more comfortable, letting the sarong flow freely, showing off the naked flesh underneath. "We have to do whatever we can to protect the name and the family."

"So how did you come across your Sir?"

"It's the Internet, silly. Anyone can collar and lead anyone nowadays, without ever having to enter the real-time community, Sir. I thought You would have figured that part out by now."

I was trying to lead her to my questions regarding her Dominant, mainly in that I wanted to know who he was, so I could get the rundown on him. "Who is the Sir you serve? Is He in the local community?"

"No, haven't You been listening?" The irritation showed on her face, and she took to the defensive, nearly shutting down on me completely. "Look, He's married and it's complicated, but it's the only real way i can satisfy my kinks for the moment, until i'm in a better position to do what i want to do. Right now, that's not possible."

I didn't care too much about the pity-party she was trying to throw and expect me to be in attendance for it. The way I saw it, that was on her to deal with the stresses of dealing with someone who didn't want to be completely honest about himself, much less his wife and presumably a family, too. I kept my focus on trying to figure out how she fit into this whole mess.

Thankfully, the Internet told on everyone, so it wouldn't be hard to figure it out. So, instead of hammering her about the phantom menace in her life, I focused on the heart of the matter. "It might come out in the next day about the person who almost killed your sister. I thought I would come by and tell you personally. The media coverage could be extensive due to the status of your parents, I figured you might want to have a prepared statement or something."

Serena's body language gave rise to her being more worried about how she could get closer and maybe get a little play time in, rather than showing any real concern over the particulars of the case. She did, however, feel the need to offer something of a theory of her own. "Sir, i appreciate You coming by to tell Me about sirius confessing to the attempted murder. Do You think some-one else put him up to it? Maybe someone who might have wanted my sister but couldn't have her?"

She tripped a wire or two with her response. First, how did she know that sirius was in custody? Second, how would she have been so intimately involved in her sister's relationship and sexual history, and why, for that matter?

The answer to my first question came in the form of the news broadcast on Fox 5 Atlanta reporting footage of sirius being taken into custody at his house, along with the information being broadcast that he was the prime suspect in the attempted murder. While they didn't give his scene name, the fact that she even knew who he was said more about her supposed lack of participation in the real-time community than anything else.

"How do you know sirius, Serena?"

"We'd seen each other at a private dungeon party at Mistress Lohyna's house a while ago." Serena sighed, making sure she didn't maintain eye contact. I waited for the inevitable punchline to the story, since it was the same story I'd heard a hundred times before. "he and i went out on a few dates before i stopped seeing him. he was a good lay, but he wasn't a Dominant."

I hated when I was right. This case was getting messier by the moment. "Lohyna is careful about the guest list at Her house. I'll have to check that out, of course."

"Of course, i wouldn't expect anything less from You, Sir." Serena's facial expression turned serious, almost like she was as invested in finding out the truth as much as I was. "i remember Kendyl telling me that Mistress and sirius were vetting each other for Her to place him under consideration. i don't know what that might have to do with my sister, but there's gotta be something there, right?"

"Yeah, but you have to know that I'm having a problem with how you know all of this information, Serena." I put my cards on the table to flush her out. She was hiding something, and it was only a matter of time before I figured it out. "Come clean and tell me what you know, or I'll be apt to suspect you in some way for what happened to your sister."

Serena looked shocked, like I'd sent a bolt of lightning through her body. After realizing that she wouldn't be able to hide anymore, she shrugged in resignation. "Okay, so i'm a bit more involved in the Atlanta scene than i led You to believe. i guess i talked too much instead of trying to seduce You, huh?"

I laughed out loud, more at her candor that she wanted to seduce me to try to throw me off the trail. She might have been able to, but she wouldn't have gotten too far. I learned my lesson while dealing with Mistress Edge, and I wasn't inclined to make the same mistake twice. "There's no way to know now, you decided not to, so it's time to come clean. And for that matter, how is it you've been able to stay off Ramesses's and Neferterri's radar all this time?"

Serena didn't hesitate in her response. "They run in a lot of circles, but the one thing i learned about Ramesses and Neferterri, it's that they rarely move in the circles i run in. i prefer to indulge in more interracial relationships, which puts me outside of their radar. The people i play with also usually play in the swingers circles a lot of the time, and Ramesses and Neferterri have been out of that scene for a while now. They might know of me through my scene name, shadow kitten, but they don't know me."

I wanted to argue the point, but the fact was that she was right. While they had a lot of friends in the Leather circles that were on the other side of the racial spectrum, they weren't as entrenched in the Euro-centric areas of the city. That's not to say they weren't well-known in those circles, either, but they had a lot to deal with when it came to the compounds and such. It made it difficult to be everywhere that people wanted them to be.

"Okay, so now that we've gotten that out of the way, why do you think that sirius and Lohyna are connected to this?"

"When we were still fucking, sirius used to talk about how Lohyna always wanted a submissive boi and girl to serve Her together, and he was convinced that She had found both, but She was going through the vetting process." Serena spun the story as she understood it, but until I could verify any of it, it was only a story. "Rumors started swirling that my sister was the one She was vetting, but Kendyl was dealing with someone else, too. Maybe Lohyna might have gotten irritated that my sister was playing both Dominants against each other to see what would be the best situation for her?"

I didn't want to give myself away at that moment, but she'd gift-wrapped a motive for Kraven to want his submissive harmed. Maybe she knew, maybe she didn't, but one thing was for certain: I had that son of a bitch dead to rights. All I needed to do was get with Lohyna to corroborate the account, get Serena to testify in court, and several birds could be killed with one stone.

Today was going to be a good day after all.

"Do Me a favor and make sure you don't have any travel plans over the next few days. I might need you to corroborate some things, for the sake of making sure an innocent man doesn't go to prison for a crime he didn't commit." I got up to leave, waiting for her to lead me to the door and let me out of her space.

She still couldn't avoid trying once more to get my attention, this time being more blatant about her intentions by unraveling the knot on her sarong and letting it fall to the floor. "Are You sure You wouldn't want to place some marks on this body, Sir? my Sir is a bit of an exhibitionist, and He loves showing off the marks I have on my body on Fet, regardless of who puts the marks on me. If You want me to beg, i have no problems begging You. Please, Sir, my body is Yours to abuse as You see fit; i beg You."

She dropped to her knees, arching her back to show off her flexibility as she presented her naked form in a position that any and everything could be done to her, without hesitation or resistance.

For a moment, I was tempted.

In the next moment, I let myself out.

She had me completely fucked up if she thought I was going to compromise myself again. Frankly speaking, I almost considered it an insult; what self-respecting Dominant would allow their submissive to do anything with anyone without vetting them first?

She's playing games, and now I was convinced more than ever that she had something going on that had her implicated in all of this. The only problem was finding out what role she played in all of this.

My cell phone rang, and I saw it was J-Roc. Things were about to get even more fun. "You got him?"

"Yeah, we got him, D."

"Good, get him to the Cage. I'll be there in an hour. Don't start the fun without me."

SEVENTEEN

"Is everything okay, Dom? You have a different aura around You from the last time You came to see Me."

The one thing I always hated about people who read auras and chakras and all of that metaphysical shit was that they could read people to the damn letter. When Neferterri did that shit to me the first time we met, I was ready to think she had some cameras in my damn house or something. Over the years, I got used to it, but that didn't exactly mean that I wanted them to do it on every given occasion, either.

There was no hiding from Lohyna, and considering I had more intense things to handle once I got back to the office, I needed to cut to the chase with the quickness. "My Lady, were You vetting Kendyl with the intention to place her under consideration?"

Lohyna wasn't the least bit surprised about my question. "I'd hoped that the connection wouldn't have come up, but yes, I was vetting diamante. she was at one of My parties a few months ago, and we engaged in a scene together. The energy between us was electric. she initially inquired about whether I would be interested in accepting her, and I couldn't resist. A couple of days later, she told me that she was in a D/s relationship with someone else, but she was trying to figure out how to separate from that relationship to be with Me."

The situation was starting to take on a life of its own now. Considering Lohyna played all her cards close to the vest, while her ex-husband was always out and proud and flaunting every possible relationship he could with the exception of Kendyl, this had the potential to get complicated from a legal perspective.

Could Kraven have found out that Kendyl was trying to leave him for his ex-wife? If that was the case, could his temper and jealousy have gotten the best of him and he had something bad happen to her? The flip side of the equation had me even more disturbed: could Lohyna have found out about Kendyl being involved with her ex-husband and had her own fit of rage, too? Especially when sirius is the connective piece to her, which could easily make her the more viable person of interest.

The thing that made the whole situation a little harder to sort through was sirius's relationships to everyone involved. He was protecting someone, that much was for certain, but the question was who, exactly? It could be Lohyna, considering the innuendo was pointing in her direction, but it could also be someone else entirely. The other thing was that he could be protecting Serena, too, but what would have been the point of that?

I was still convinced of my original premise that landed Kraven's sociopathic streak squarely in the crosshairs of the suspicions I had about who had something to do with the harm that was caused to Kendyl.

I had to take my emotions out of the situation to be able to figure this out objectively, and the only way I would be able to do that was to have the chance to freestyle at home or in my office where I could have a clearer head. Having the girls with me would help out even more, to have them as sounding boards.

Lohyna got into a bit of a monologue, waxing poetic about her history, almost like she was pining away for a time gone by. "When I met Neal, I was in a dark place. I was sick of the scene in Houston;

I'd just gotten out of a bad relationship with a guy who I thought was able to be real with Me. I almost thought I was destined to be alone...and then I met Him."

I sat down next to her, trying to listen more closely to what she was saying. What I'd learned while on the force was that when people were at their most vulnerable, they were also their most authentic. The truth felt like a weight being lifted from the soul during those moments, and I wanted desperately to have that truth set her free, while simultaneously burying her ex-husband, once and for all.

"I knew everything He was being accused of before I got with Him, but like most fools, I took the attitude of 'He didn't do anything to Me, so it doesn't matter what He did; it's all hearsay anyway.'" I saw the tears falling from her eyes as the pains of the past began to show themselves clearly in hindsight. "I was so engrossed by His presence, His money, His influence in business circles...I chose to be blinded by the truth. The things that He did; the things I chose not to see that caused us to leave the one place I could call home before we came to Atlanta. Do You ever feel like You have time to make things right, Dominic?"

That question shook me to my core. All the time I put in with the department, all the times when I felt like I was making a difference, only to realize that I wasn't doing anything for anyone. Everything came flooding back into my mind from places that I thought I'd locked away from my consciousness. I didn't know how to answer her question; the one thing that came rushing to the surface was the time that was robbed from me to make things right with Sherrie.

Lohyna looked entranced, not caring whether I answered her questions or not. She continued to purge, each word looking like links in the chain that were breaking as she spoke them into existence. Words that no longer held her hostage as she continued to garner the strength to free herself. "I didn't want to think He was a bad man, didn't want to think that He was the monster that the ones who hated him most thought He was. He still had His fan club; You know how it is in the community. But at the end of the day, I chose to be with Him. I'm not sure if I regret it now or not, but I know I have as much to blame in a lot of what happened by not saying anything. I'll have to live with that until I leave this existence."

"My Lady, what's done is done. What You can do is help a girl who, I assume, was as much into You as You were into her." I found my voice, using it to my best advantage while she was amiable and compliant. "I can't prove that Your ex had something to do with what happened to diamante, but I think You can help me. Will you help Me, My Lady? Maybe You can find some redemption for those other girls You couldn't find the strength to help by doing this now? Please?"

Lohyna turned to me, wiping the tears from her eyes and offering a smile that shone brighter than the merciless summer sun we were trying to keep from being scorched by. "Dominic, I will do whatever it takes to help You. If I find out He had anything to do with what happened to My diamante, I'll bury Him before You get the chance to arrest Him."

EIGHTEEN

"AHHHHHHHHHHHH!!!! YOU CAN'T DO THIS!!!!! ARR-RGGGGHHHHHH!!!!"

All I had to do was follow the screams and thuds down to the Cage and I would find out everything I needed to know about what was about to go down with Kraven's wannabe heavy who called himself threatening Neferterri and the girls.

The reason I said he was a wannabe was simple: he really wasn't about that life. One look at him from the pictures that V12 sent to me and I could tell he wasn't about that life. He looked like Jason Bateman but without hair, and Jason Bateman could never be confused with being a hard-core badass. If anything, he had no business being in Kraven's employ, but soon we would all find out the backstory. There was always a backstory.

After I left Lohyna's house, I stopped by the house to check on them, ensuring them that Kraven's efforts would not go unnoticed or without reprisal, either. It was best to have them all at one location from a logistical standpoint; we didn't want to have resources stretched too thin in case Kraven decided that he thought he was the second coming of Al Capone. Ramesses was a lot of things, but when it came to his family, D/s or otherwise, he was part Rottweiler, part Pharaoh hound, and no force on earth would be able to stop him. That was the reason for the Ghost Squad protocol in the first place: to keep him from getting his hands dirty.

Neferterri was pissed that she had to even go through the protective detail to begin with. She was probably more hot-tempered than her husband was; the difference between them was she didn't give two fucks if she unleashed her anger. Ramesses was the more diplomatic of the two, but he was an unmovable object when it came to the safety of the people in his life. Hell, he even had someone keeping an eye on amani, their male submissive. Based on the incident that happened on the private island last year, I knew he could handle himself if someone tried to come for him, but again, what the Master of the House wanted, the Master of the House got.

shamise and sajira didn't mind the detail too much. With those two, they saw the extra protection as romantic; they were wired funny like that, and knowing shamise, she would have them entertained and occupied in such a fashion that they wouldn't mind following them anywhere they wanted to go.

Remember that nonsense I was tripping about with the GPS trackers? I understood the method to his madness once I saw all the trackers showing up on the radar in Ramesses's office. The ultimate security measure, but something that took the ultimate sacrifice of trust and privacy. That's not something to be taken lightly, but considering all of the submissives had been branded and collared, I didn't think a silly thing like a tracking chip implanted under the skin would be asking too much. Even the kids were tagged.

I wasn't on that level yet, but I damn sure wanted to be in time.

Before I headed over to Lohyna's house, I was with Ramesses getting the information on the "threat." Turned out, he wasn't much of a threat at all. His name was Tom Logan; typical name for someone who, like I said, was trying to be about that life, but didn't have what it took to be about that life. He didn't even have enough presence of mind to at least get rid of the burner he used, but it didn't take much to find him anyway. He thought we wouldn't be able to find him, or at least, that's what his handler must have told him.

Bad career move, partner.

The way he ended up getting caught was almost comical; he stayed around the area where he made the call. Another rookie mistake, and I probably was sounding like a broken record, but he wasn't about that life. When they found him, as I understand it, he stuck out like a sore thumb; about six feet three inches, bald with a goatee and mustache, but he was slightly built, and easy to take. According to Illmatic, one of the other boys on the Squad, Logan almost shit his clothes when he approached.

Considering they picked him up in Duluth, yeah, that might have had something to do with it.

J-Roc couldn't stop laughing over the phone as he gave me the rundown on what happened on the drive back to the office. He said Logan tried to bribe them with the money he got for doing the gig. When I found out how much the job was for, I almost wanted to laugh myself, but that would be cruel. Kraven must have been in dire straits to pull bargain-basement pricing to get this fool, or dude was that far out of sorts that he was willing to do it for the low like that. Five thousand dollars? Come on, son!

That would almost be an insult, and on top of that, he didn't even get the job done right.

The scene in front of me once I got into the Cage, it looked like I had missed a lot of the action. That was fine; it looked like Sigma was warming up with some of the things he was using to get the guy to talk. If I wondered why Ramesses wanted Sigma brought in for this, I didn't have to wonder anymore. Dude had tools and moved like Huck from *Scandal*, except he wasn't all stalker-creepy-looking and shit like that.

Sigma wasted no time getting into the questions he needed to ask, and from the way dude was screaming, the answers would come fast and furious. "I'm sure you're wondering how this is going to work, and I'm inclined to oblige you. I'm going to ask questions, and you're going to answer them. My boss wants to know who sent you for him, and before you decide to want to be all hero and such—"

Sigma took a bolt cutter and clipped off Logan's index finger like it was made out of cardboard. Hearing the bone crunch and then snap was enough to make me want to hurl, but I kept myself in check, even though blood spurted from the open wound. The howl from him was ear-piercing; it was easy to guess that he was definitely going to sing the blues, whether he wanted to or not.

"So, now that you know I'm serious, who sent you?"

"Oh, fuck, you cut my finger off!"

"Focus, Logan, or you'll see another one come off just as quickly. Who sent you?"

Logan took deep breaths, glaring at Sigma once he had a chance to calm down a little from the initial pain surge. That didn't take long, as Sigma went for the middle finger of the hand where he'd severed the index finger. Logan yelled for him not to cut the other finger, but it was too late. This time, he screamed out for dear life, the bass in his voice damn near gone at this point. If he kept this up, he was bound not to have too many fingers left, if he didn't bleed out first.

"You're stubborn, I'll give you that, but I'm not the patient type, and I'm not wrapped too tight when I'm in situations like this, so, I'm going to ask you one last time…who was the person who sent you to threaten my boss?" Sigma was still calm and stone-cold serious about every word he was saying to Logan. "Now, before you go into shock, it might be in your best interest to go ahead and give me the answer I want. It might mean the difference between you going home patched up or you going home to glory. Which one would you prefer?"

"All right, all right! Segal is his name, dammit! He told me the guy wouldn't do anything to me, that all I had to do was threaten him and make it sound convincing." Logan did what he could to talk while he still had the wherewithal to do so. The look in his eyes gave him away; he was fading fast, and he was certain to lose consciousness. "He wanted the guy I threatened to drop his pursuit of some case against him or something. That's all I know, fuck…I'm serious, that's all I know!"

Sigma took the bolt cutter and began wiping the blood off the blades. He grabbed the first aid kit nearby and began to tend to the open wounds. It was like the monster that he had turned into moments before had switched off or something. "It's a shame that you had to lose an extra finger because you just insisted on being so stubborn, Mr. Logan. It's one thing to explain to your boss how you lost one finger, but two? It's going to be a real doozy of a story, I think."

Before too long, the rest of the Squad had the area cleaned and cleared out like nothing had happened in the hours before. Sigma walked over to where Ramesses and I stood, maintaining eye contact the entire time he stood there. "I wasn't sure how quickly he would give up the name, but I figured after J-Roc told me what happened in the van, I didn't think I would have to break a sweat. He should be fine, though; I'm not sure what your endgame would be to keep him from talking. He obviously wasn't built for this."

Ramesses took a look at Logan, stroking his beard as he normally did when he needed to ponder something. It couldn't have been much to ponder; based on the information we dug up on him, he was nothing more than a nomad, with no family ties whatsoever. No one in the city would miss him, we were sure of that, which also meant Kraven was as sure as we were of that fact. That was a cause for concern in my mind; he might be on to our methods, and that was something I couldn't allow.

Ramesses's cell phone rang. When he checked the caller ID, a perplexed look showed up on his face. "Kraven, such a coincidence that you're calling me. Is there something that I can do for you?"

"Ramesses, I believe the proper question to ask is, given the circumstances, what can you do to help yourself out of a rather fine mess you've gotten yourself into?" Kraven's voice sounded nearly as smug as he did earlier when I ran into him at the police station. "After all, you're putting yourself at great risk with the moves that you're making against me. You might find yourself losing a great deal more coming after me."

Ramesses placed the phone near where Logan was still writhing in pain and whimpering, so Kraven could get an earful of what took place. "Does it sound like I'm worried about the consequences of making moves against you, Kraven? This piece of shit you hired threatened to come after my wife and our submissives. You might find yourself losing a great deal more trying to play gangster."

"Oh, you think I'm playing gangster, Sir?" Kraven had gone from smug to dismissive, nearly laughing over the phone at what he perceived as an empty threat. "You don't get to where I've gotten without learning a few things and picking up some friends in low places. Did you ever think for a moment that I might have planted that piss-poor excuse for a hit man out there for you to collect and torture? That man means nothing to me, and I'll prove it."

Ramesses and I looked at each other for a second or two, glancing over at Sigma as he'd already read between the lines of what Kraven was driving at.

The next thing we knew, Logan began to seize, frothing at the mouth and going into convulsions. Sigma rushed to where he lay, trying to administer CPR and calm the convulsions as best he could, but in a couple of minutes, Sigma shook his head, and all we heard was the sickening laughter of an absolute nutcase.

"Oh my goodness, I wish I could be there to see your faces right now. That was a poison I had him ingest, under the guise of alcohol that he wanted to drink before he went through with the phone call he made to you. I knew he was yellow, but damn." Kraven couldn't contain his amusement. "Now, if you're really wanting to play this game, Ramesses, I suggest you throw away that decorum of yours. It won't get you anywhere, and it might get someone else killed, if you're not careful."

Realizing that Logan was the only real connection we had to Kraven's threats against Ramesses, there was no way we could really go after him on legalities. Even the skip trace that was recording the conversation wouldn't completely hold up in court. The case would be paper-thin, and he might be able to countersue for defamation, which could put the compounds at risk. There was silence on our end as we tried to quietly figure out what the next move was.

Sigma felt something for a moment, and once he looked down, he silently got my attention. I signaled to Ramesses what the new development was, and once he got a quick glimpse, he gave the thumbs-up signal and allowed the rest of the monologue to continue.

"See, that's the problem with you, Ramesses, you have a code that you have to live by. That's what makes you vulnerable and weak." Kraven continued to spout off at the mouth. "It makes you really predictable, which was how I was able to set things up with ol' Tom down there. He was the perfect mark, and he was expendable, too. If I really wanted to be cutthroat, I could have done something much more devastating, if I wanted to."

I wanted badly to wipe the look on his face that I imagined he had. He honestly thought he had the upper hand. I was wondering if he had the balls to actually try to be a badass in person, instead of trying to play hard over the phone. I saw his file, studied it in its entirety: he truly wasn't about that life. He had the money to look the part, but he didn't have the connections that he thought he had. "Paper Don" was the exact description I had for his behavior.

Kraven decided to try and add insult to injury, trying to go for the jugular. "Of course, all of this can go away without issue if you simply drop the case. I'd hate for something bad to happen to NEBU; I really like the place. It couldn't be anywhere nearly as popular as it could be if you allowed some of the other elements into the membership, but I guess no situation is perfect."

Ramesses wasn't in the mood for games anymore; he needed to cut to the chase, and so did I. The veiled threat toward his "baby" was the last straw. "So, how exactly are you planning to end this so-called game we're playing, Sir? I'm curious to know, seeing as you think you've already beaten me at this point."

"I can tell you now, I have beaten you."

"Not when I still have the audio of the call in my possession." Ramesses didn't want to show all of his cards, but he also wanted to rattle his cage a little bit. "I'm sure that the ADA would love to know what other indiscretions you might be accountable for. You know, in the interests of justice and all? I'm sure you wouldn't mind that at all."

"And you also have the carcass of the other person in your possession, too. Did I neglect to mention that I hadn't paid him yet?" Kraven laughed again, but this time, I wasn't fazed by his laughter. He'd hooked himself without us offering the bait anymore. "You're going to have a hard time getting that pretty little ADA of yours to press charges with such flimsy evidence."

He sounded a little disturbed in that last exchange, like he might have realized that we might have something else on him that he wasn't exactly accounting for. His voice wasn't as full of confidence as it was at the beginning of the call.

Ramesses must have recognized it, too; the hesitation in his voice emboldened him. But, in typical Ramesses fashion, he left his opponent in the dark and guessing over what his next move might be. Ever the chess player. "Well, there's only one way to find out, Sir, seeing as you have the upper hand in this situation. I'd hate to upset you or cause you to try to capitalize on that advantage, either. In the meantime, I wouldn't want to make any long-range trips out of town, though. I also wouldn't be surprised if we don't see you in the next day or so. Oh, one more thing: there's still the matter of your threats against my wife and our submissives. If I were you, I would seriously be looking over my shoulder for the foreseeable future. You were better off coming for me like a man instead of threatening my family. Now, I'm going to make it my personal business that your whole world comes to a screeching halt."

Ramesses cut the phone off before Kraven could retort. It was a good thing, too; Sigma was having one hell of a time keeping Logan's screams and whimpers from reaching the speakerphone. "Is he still alert, Sigma?"

"Yes, Sir, he is."

"Good." Ramesses walked over to him, kneeled down next to him as Sigma continued to apply the pressure to his wounds to keep him from blacking out. His eyes locked with Logan's, as to make sure he was heard clearly when he spoke to him. "You're going to disappear, do you hear me?"

Logan nodded, feeling the effects of the sedative Sigma used. What he wasn't aware of was the concoction was a combination of Rohypnol and a few other narcotics that would have him waking up about twelve hours from now, completely unaware of where he was—outside of the hospital he would end up in somewhere in north Florida—and what happened to him. The explanation of his severed fingers was also a fabrication, a recount that would be told to the emergency personnel after he was dropped off with them: he was in the process of saving a young child from falling into a well, and he got his hand stuck against some sharp rocks. He ripped his hand away, severing his fingers in the process, passing out from the loss of blood. He wouldn't want any publicity over the act; all he needed was a chance to get on his feet again.

That story would work out better than the one that his former employer had in store for him. Somehow I doubted that he even cared if Logan was dead or alive; if he did, he would have at least come to check for himself at the very least, instead of thinking that the poison took him out.

Logan slipped into the darkness, his body going limp as the sedative finally took its hold on his body. In the next moment, he was being loaded into J-Roc's truck, heading to Peachtree-DeKalb Airport, where a plane was waiting for his arrival and subsequent departure. Destination: Tampa.

Once he disappeared, I turned to Ramesses, shaking my head at the whole situation. "Kraven's trying to play dirty, partner. When do you plan to get grimy with him?"

"I don't have to get grimy, partner," Ramesses replied, taking his phone out to make another call. "That's what I have you for; to make me look good. However, he's not getting away with that bullshit threat against Neferterri and the girls. I'm going to make his life a living hell, you can believe that shit. The only time that I plan to do anything whatsoever about Kraven is once I have his balls to the wall and he can't go anywhere or use anyone else to slip out of another charge. When he slips up—and he already has slipped up—I'm going to nail him, you can take that to the bank."

NINETEEN

The next morning brought its own brand of madness, which was something I was hoping would not be the case, but the way these cases were set up, there was no avoiding the inevitability.

The first instance of trouble on the horizon was the call from Niki. It wasn't good; sirius had been charged with kidnapping and attempted murder. The Ashtons wanted a quick resolution to the mess, and Kraven had managed to place himself in the midst of the situation, almost to the point to where he almost came out looking like the hero. As it turned out, that was the sole reason he came down to the precinct when we crossed paths.

What I wanted to know was how in the world he was able to identify sirius as the suspect so easily? He wasn't anywhere in the vicinity of the crime or where the body ended up being deposited, so how in the world was he able to be the shining hero in this scenario? This thing was beginning to stink; the politics demanded that someone was going to take the rap for this, and it looked like they were able to find the scapegoat for this particular crime. My old captain would have never let me roll with the flimsy evidence and the suspect identification, but I had to remember that I wasn't with my old captain, and this crime happened in a different part of the city—the part that was financially influential.

This nightmare couldn't have played out any worse. With Kraven acting like he was instrumental in the capture of the suspect, it made it that much more difficult to figure out if he had anything to do with what happened to Kendyl. I was incensed, and for good reason; there's no telling what the hell he told the ADAs assigned to the case, and Niki wouldn't be able to tell me anything while she was at the office or risk conflict of interest and recusal.

sirius was being railroaded. Everything that was happening further fueled my suspicions that he was covering for someone, and it was becoming clearer by the minute that the person was Kraven, but the connection between the two escaped my grasp. Kraven didn't deal with male submissives on that type of level; in fact, I was certain he had a contempt for them to the degree that they weren't even allowed in his presence at public functions.

This whole situation was working my nerves. I needed to figure out what in the bloody hell was going on before the wrong person got pinned for something that I knew for a fact he didn't do.

In the middle of my stressing out over this case, I got a call from Ty out of the blue, which was a godsend to say the least. I had been waiting on his call for a couple of days now, hopeful that he would be able to figure some things out on the virtual end with regard to the other case involving Jason and Tori. "Ty, give me some good news, bro."

"I can do better than that, bro, I can show you a hell of a lot of stuff, including your killer." Ty sounded really hyper, almost nervously excited for some reason, and he didn't usually sound that way. "Can you get over here, ASAP? I think you'll be *very* interested in what I have to show you. It's definitely some explosive stuff."

Now, as long as I'd known Ty, he'd always been cooler than the other side of the pillow, to borrow the phrase from the late, great Stuart Scott, so to hear him sounding a little more animated than usual was a warning sign for me. Either someone was there with him, or they'd been there and given him the scare of his life.

I decided to test my theory so I would know how to prepare when I got over there. "Ty, how explosive is the information? Is it righteous, or is it to die for?"

"It's definitely to die for, D." He used the phrase I thought he would use. The killer was still there with him, and the coded phrases we were using were meant to keep Ty alive more than anything, but there was no guarantee that he would be alive once I got there. I was betting on the idea that the killer wanted to catch a big fish with live bait than the alternative.

Time was of the essence, and I made that clear to him while I had him on the phone. "Give me twenty minutes to get over there, bro. I have a feeling this might be the break I'm looking for in this case."

I hung up the phone, grabbing for my guns as I headed out the door. Something was off, and I had a feeling that if I didn't get to Ty soon, I would run into a scene that I wouldn't be able to handle.

I got to Ty's house by dusk, and my senses were already heightened by the time I pulled up to the house.

I purposely parked the unmarked sedan I drove a couple of houses away from his, as to not trip out the person that I suspected lay in wait for me, using Ty as bait for a convenient trap that I had no choice but to walk into. I had no idea whether Ty was dead or alive, but I couldn't let a friend go without a fight. I'd completely dropped the ball with Tori, and I was not about to make the same mistake twice.

Neither of them would have recognized the car as I drove past, so I still had the element of surprise on my side. That might have been the only advantage I had as I quietly slipped to the front door. I grabbed a handkerchief from my pocket, using it to cover my prints. I checked the door and hoped that my instincts weren't on point.

Unfortunately, they were, as the door opened with little effort.

Keep your head, Law. You know he's in here somewhere.

The lights were out; not a good sign.

He wanted me to know he was here. The question I had that hadn't been answered was whether Ty was here, and if he was still breathing.

I cleared each room in his townhome, going through the ground floor first. His place had three floors, and considering he was as careful as I was, he had cameras everywhere, with night vision capabilities in case someone got the bright idea that nothing could be seen in the dark.

My advantage had now become my disadvantage. For all I knew, the killer was here in the house with Ty, watching me as I cleared the house. Rather than trying to give the clue that I knew where to go, I continued clearing each room, eventually moving to the second floor to do the same thing.

This cat-and-mouse game that was being played irritated me to no end, and I wanted to get this over with, but I couldn't simply do that without tipping my adversary off and making him do something rash. I had to play this to its conclusion, no matter how much my nerves wanted me to end the curiosity and cut to the heart of the matter. Ty's life was at stake.

After clearing the second floor, I made my way to the third floor, knowing where the control room was, but playing stupid the whole way. I kept trying to calm my irritation, wondering where they were, not in the mood for the hide-and-seek games any longer. My mind prepared for a fight, and it would only be a matter of time before I got what I wanted. It wasn't a matter of if, but when.

I finally heard a hint of Ty, hearing him groaning in one of the side bedrooms across from the control room. I moved to where I heard the sounds coming from, finding him bruised and bloodied, but still alive, thankfully.

I checked his vitals, finding a faint pulse as I turned him on his back to let him know I was there with him. "Don't worry, bro, I need you to hang tight until I take care of this dude. Can you get to the silent alarm and trip it?"

"Yeah…I think so…I don't know where he went…he…he might be…hiding somewhere." Ty was having a hard time breathing, and it might have been asking a lot, but I figured I would be able to keep the killer busy long enough for Ty to make his way to the alarm in the control room. "He's crazy, Dom…it's like he's possessed or something…you can't take him straight up."

"Don't worry about me, bro; just get to the alarm so the cops can get here." I rose from where he was to check the rest of the top floor.

I kept my gun drawn, my senses alerting me that someone was still close by. I yelled out into the darkness, taunting him while trying to keep my anger at bay over what had been done to my friend. "You had to be a bitch and beat on someone who couldn't defend himself, huh? How about you come for someone your own size, jackass!"

I heard a sound coming from the bathroom, and I moved in that direction as quickly as I could, tracking the sound to the bathroom closet. I moved to a position to where I could get the drop on him, staying low to avoid any head shots, in case he had a gun, too.

"Okay, hide and seek is over, bitch, and I don't want to have to stain my friend's linen or clothing, so come out nice and slow, and I won't have to put a bullet in the door to put you out of your misery."

I moved a little closer, passing by the bathtub, doing a quick swipe across the shower curtain to feel if someone might have been standing in the tub. My patience was short; under normal circumstances, I wouldn't have been so sloppy. Convinced that he was in the closet, I moved away from the tub, fixating my attention back in that direction. My pulse quickened; I couldn't figure out which way I wanted to move, but I needed to end this as quickly as possible. I tried to decide between the kill shot or pulling him out so I could see him for myself.

A few seconds later, my patience had run out. "I'm counting to three, and I'm putting a bullet in the door. One…two…"

I didn't get to three.

He came out of the shower, swinging and connecting with the back of my head. I felt cold steel as I instantly saw colors. Brass knuckles; he was a bitch, and a cheater, too. I dropped to one knee, dropping my gun in reflex as he tried to connect with my head again in an attempt to knock me out.

I slipped the second swing, swiping my elbow behind me and connected with his ribcage, causing him to cry out in pain. My eyes were still a little blurry from the first strike, so I had to rely on his sounds to let me know how close he was to me. I followed the elbow with a hard right cross to the same area, hoping to stun him until my vision cleared, but this guy seemed to be on as much adrenaline as I was. He recovered quickly, landing a series of blows to my jaw that should have put me down quick, but my fight-or-flight instincts were purely in survival mode.

I lunged at him to avoid the punches to my face, driving him into the wall near the sink. He seemed to be ready for me with that move, too, as he drove an elbow into my lower back before dropping a knee into my shoulder that launched me away from him and into the door of the closet.

He was on me in seconds, pinning my shoulder with his knee and commencing to pummel my ribcage, the wild look in his eyes giving me the distinct impression that he was going to try to kill me, one way or the other. I tried to use my free arm to counter and slow him down, but he seemed possessed, like nothing I did affected him at all.

Ty was right; I wasn't ready, and he was taking full advantage of the fact that I wasn't ready.

I was determined to not have him beat me to death, so in a desperate move, I lifted my knee and got him flush in his groin. The pain shot through him like he'd been struck by lightning, the howl sounding like a banshee in the night air as he rolled off me. I still had some fight left in me, and now that I had the upper hand for a moment, I picked myself off the ground, holding my ribs as I stalked him, insistent on dropping him permanently for making me work to find him and putting me through this shit.

A swift leg sweep took me off my feet, and the way I landed on the tile floor knocked the wind out of me. He took the same leg he swept me with and dropped it across my bruised ribs, making it harder to breathe.

He had the drop on me, and with my gun within arm's reach, he could have easily picked it up and put me out of my misery. I did what I could to get up, but every time I moved, it made it harder to breathe. He saw me stretch out for my gun, stepping over me to kick it out of my reach. Realizing he had me beat, he proceeded to slap my face over and over, trying to humiliate me. I couldn't lift my left arm; he'd managed to stretch it to where I had no strength to do any real damage to him.

"Pathetic. I thought you would give me a better fight. I don't know what my Mistress saw in you." He continued to slap my face, no longer worried about me coming for him again. I was nearly unconscious from the lack of oxygen in my system. I struggled for every bit of air I could get. "I'm gonna make you pay for killing my Mistress. I'll make you all pay dearly."

Killing his Mistress? Did he mean Kacie? She was dead?

My mind swirled as the words hit my ears. I thought I was hearing things; the last time I'd checked on her, she was still in the same prison that Simone was housed in. She had been transferred from the Emmanuel Correctional facility in South Georgia after she got caught having sex with one of the guards and causing harm to another inmate. Needless to say, she was no longer considered a candidate for minimal security facilities.

There was no way she could have been killed while she was down there. I knew Sarge too well; he would have never allowed something like that to happen on his watch.

He spat in my face, the ultimate disrespect. The glare in his eyes let me know that he could have ended me if he wanted to, but something else in his eyes tipped me off as to why he couldn't. Someone was controlling him. But who?

He took one more swing, fading my world to black with a punch to my temple. The last sound I heard was the security system's speakers, asking Ty if he needed assistance. He was able to trip the system while I was getting my ass handed to me.

At least someone would find us before too long, but I knew a few people that wouldn't be too happy to see me laid up in the hospital, though.

I wouldn't be in there for long. There was no way in hell he was getting away with this. I didn't care if I had to raze half the city; I was going to find him and get some payback. In one defiant statement, he admitted to killing Tori, and he was planning to kill everyone else who had a hand in putting Kacie away, which led to her unfortunate demise.

There was something deeper going on, and I was determined to find out what the hell it was. He wasn't about to have the last word, as long as I had breath in my body, that was not about to be the case.

This wasn't over by a long shot.

TWENTY

"Damn, bruh, if you look like this, I want to know what happened to the other guy."

Ramesses, Niki and Natasha were in my room at Northside Hospital, trying to get a gauge of my injuries. He called himself trying to make a joke in light of how bad I must have looked to the three of them. Niki looked like she was ready to hunt the man down and take matters into her own hands, and Natasha's face betrayed her also, as they both tried to tell me that they weren't worried about my injuries.

Despite my need to try and dissuade their collective concerns, the truth was that I felt like I'd been hit by a semi. I was groggy from the morphine drip, but I wasn't too far gone to find out the answer to one very important question. "Is Ty okay? Did he make it?"

"Yes, my Sir, Ty is okay, thanks to You." Natasha beamed as she recounted the story that Ty told her once he regained consciousness. "He said You took a beating, but You managed to cause enough bleeding for forensics to get a profile on Your attacker."

That was the first bit of good news I'd heard since I woke up. I sat up in the bed, putting my hand out in expectation of getting the file that would tell me everything I needed to know about this mystery man. She smiled as she placed the file in my hand, blushing as our eyes met briefly.

As I perused the file, I rattled off the bullet points to share with the rest of the group. "Hmmm, dude's name is Karrion, and he used to be in a D/s relationship with Edge before her death."

"Wait a minute, did you say death?" Ramesses stopped me before I could get started with the presentation. "When did Edge die?"

"Apparently, that happened about a week before Jason was killed." I didn't like where this particular road was going to lead me, but I had no choice but to follow things to their conclusion. "I have a feeling that dude was planted into our circle with the express purpose of getting revenge on us for the death of his Mistress."

"Sir, it has to be something a little less simplistic than coming after us for Edge's downfall." Niki felt like this was a matter of being petty. She turned to Natasha, who nodded in her agreement of the initial assessment. "What happened to the instructions to keep her isolated once she was transferred? Did they ignore those orders or something?"

They had a point, and there was no denying that somehow the protocol at the prison was circumvented, but the multitude of questions seemed to never end. Who breached protocol? How did it happen? The questions kept coming, and the more they flooded my mind, the more my head hurt.

"Sarge was the point of contact for everything I wanted to do at Pulaski; I'll have to start with him." The issue I had with that suggestion was that I had to ask some hard questions for a trusted friend and former supervisor. Even more so, did I have it within me to ask those questions and demand honest answers?

"Our old sergeant is running things at Pulaski?" Niki's ears perked up over that revelation. "i might need to have a word with him, my Sir. i mean no offense, but Your relationship with him might cloud things a bit."

"Negative, Ms. Santiago." I had to get into professional character quickly to match my submissive's demeanor quickly. "Sergeant

Lynch will hear your voice and know that something's amiss. At least he knows Me and can trust Me long enough to get the answers I need from him. you're going to have to trust Me."

Ramesses chimed in before Niki could offer a rebuttal. "He's right, Madame ADA; you know how the corrections department is about anyone who might resemble anything closer to the Internal Affairs department. If anything, the familiarity has already bred trust. Allow your Sir to use this advantage to get what is needed to close this case out."

Niki considered her options, realizing that she was in a difficult position. On the other hand, she needed this case solved before anyone else within the circle was hurt or killed. "Okay, my Sir, You have the point on this one, but i need you to figure this out as discreetly as you can. This isn't a sanctioned operation by the DA's office, but i'm trusting You to do what You do, and do it quickly."

I picked up my cell phone, giving a nod to my partner, who made a call to Taliah, still in the office awaiting instructions. A few clicks later, and my phone was set up for recording from the system at the office, in case he tried to be quiet during the call. I didn't take any chances, and I wasn't about to start now.

Niki and Natasha stayed in the background, listening in on my end of the conversation, silently feeding me follow-up questions when necessary.

I was calm for a minute, until Sarge popped up on the call. All bets were off. "Dom, to what do I owe the pleasure of this call?"

"Sarge, I have to ask some hard questions of you with regard to an inmate that was killed while in your custody." I did my best to frame the interrogation in the manner that I wanted it, to keep him off balance as much as I could. I knew I was treading thin ice with the opening line, but I wasn't exactly an experienced attorney, not like Niki was. "What protocol was followed with inmate #2731034?"

"What is this about, Dom?" His paranoia sensors were already on high alert, and the pitch in his voice changed immediately. "You know protocol is paramount at the prison. What are you driving at?"

"I'm going to put this out there for you to deal with one way or another, especially considering the way you had to retire from the force to begin with." I saw Niki try to guide me to the proper line of questioning, but she wasn't aware of the information I had in my back pocket, in case he tried to be evasive about what I was asking about. "I'm trying to not put you in a compromising position, but you're going to leave me no choice in about five seconds."

"I don't know what the hell you're talking about."

"Three hundred thousand, in three separate installments, exactly three weeks apart from each other, with the last deposit made the week that the inmate in question was safely transferred to your facility."

"Come again?" Sarge's tone came up differently this time; it was uncertainty over how I knew about the amounts that I'd come up with.

"We can play dirty, Sarge, if that's what you want. I had your financials pulled after I'd realized there was a pattern of prisoner abuse in your facility, sir." I felt like I was going to lose it at any minute. "That inmate I referred to wasn't the first one, and she won't be the last one, either. Am I correct in that assumption, or should I make a call up the chain to someone else who picked up the rest of the six-figure payment for services rendered?"

The phone went silent for a few moments, a dead giveaway that the hunch I had, as much as I wanted to not believe it, had paid off. I looked at my girls, and Niki's face was priceless; she was curious to know how I had that information on hand like that.

Sarge finally huffed over the phone, resigned to deal with the line of questioning I had for him. "I always hated that you were smarter than most, Dom. I took the payment from an interested party to have that inmate transferred to me. Once she was here, she was unfortunately caught up in an altercation with another inmate, which led to her death. So, now that you've got the information, are you gonna bury me with it?"

"I didn't when you got bounced from Fulton, and I'm not going to do it now." I felt like I wanted to strangle him with my bare hands. Blood was on his hands and he didn't know it yet. He was about to now. "Who paid you to bypass protocol and put that inmate in danger?"

Sarge was incredulous. He struggled to understand what the significance was, and he articulated that confusion. "I don't get it, Dom; what is the significance of this one inmate to you? Was she a former fuck buddy of yours or something?"

I wasn't completely happy with the snide joke he threw in there with regard to my relationship with Kacie, but I kept myself in check as best I could. "You might have accepted a payment that put certain things in motion that you might not be aware of, Sarge. You cooperate, I keep my mouth shut, are we clear?"

"Fine. Yes, I took a payments to look the other way. The woman that we put her with was supposed to be a low-security risk; there was no way to know she would do what she did to her."

He was speaking in riddles and vague innuendo, and I didn't like it. I was in too much pain to drag this out too far. "This isn't about you anymore, Sarge; two people are dead, and I almost lost my own life because of whatever you allowed to happen up there. I'm stuck in a fucking hospital room because of you!"

"All I cared about was the money, I didn't give a fuck about the consequences, as long as they didn't affect me personally. What the fuck did you want me to do, tell the bitch no? Fuck you, D!"

Things were getting personal too fast. I had to find a way to regain some emotional control over him, but the meds in my system had other plans in mind. "Sarge, I need you to focus for me, understand? Who sent the money? Who was the inmate you housed her with?"

"If you think for a minute that I'm going to answer that question, you have another goddamned thing coming." Sarge dug in his heels, determined to make this a fight that I didn't have the energy for. The meds were starting to work again, and I needed answers before I was too loopy to understand the words coming out of my mouth. "They'll kill me and everyone who was in on the situation."

"Not if I don't get to you first. You won't live long enough to enjoy a penny of that money until you tell me what I want to know."

"You're in the hospital; you can't do a damn thing to me right now." Sarge laughed in my face, nearly taunting me with the information he knew. "I could tell you who was in the cell, but I have a feeling if you sit down and think long enough, you'll know who was behind her murder."

The alarm that went off in my head felt like I was in the bell tower of the Notre Dame Cathedral as the clock struck midnight. If I hadn't been so damn stupid trying to outsmart myself, I would have figured this stupid shit out to begin with. Niki's eyes widened, and I wondered if she'd reached the same conclusion that I had.

"Why did you put her in the cell with that woman? What was the endgame for doing something so careless? What the hell is that about?"

"Someone wanted your smug ass to pay for something you did, and quite frankly, I didn't flinch when your name came up in the conversation." Sarge's sneer could be felt over the earpiece, and I swore I heard him try to stifle a laugh. "The minute you got that shield, you were no longer one of us, Law. You turned your back on me, on our old unit, and for what? To go play P.I.? What kind of fantasy shit is that?"

I was getting really sick of that tired theme following me wherever I went. The fucked-up part was, if they were given the same opportunity, they would have jumped on it in a heartbeat. They all could spare me the moral indignation. "So, you felt the need to try to burn me, meanwhile innocent people had to get killed over some bullshit?"

"You might want to check yourself, Dom. I still haven't told you who your killer is."

"You don't have to tell me who it is. She's been helping me this entire time, and playing me the whole fucking time. I don't need you anymore, Sarge. I'll see you behind bars before you can blink twice." I hung up the phone before he could say another word, turning to my girls for clarification. "Was that enough for a warrant?"

"Consider him and his supervisor handled within the hour, my Sir." Niki shook her head at the sheer arrogance on display. "I knew he was grimy, but to cause someone's death and cover it up? I hope they scorch their asses!"

I was more upset at being played yet again by someone who thought I was too stupid to figure out that she had something to do with the situation that had befallen me.

I began to get out of the bed, trying to take off the IV line and ignoring the pain I felt with each smaller movement.

Ramesses looked like he was about to have me committed for losing my sanity. "I know You don't think You're going anywhere in Your condition."

"My condition is more soreness than any broken bones, Sir. I have a bitch to shake down, big time." Yes, he was my mentor, business partner, and more importantly, my friend, but he was about to catch hellfire if he wasn't careful. "She thinks she played Me from the word go, and I aim to make her pay in ways that she has no clue about."

Natasha looked at Niki, nodded like they had the same thought, and moved to press her hand against my chest. "You're not going anywhere, my Sir, not until the doctor says You can leave, and no sooner. We can pick up from here for a day while You get some rest and heal."

"And before You protest, my Sir, You're going to have to remember that You're no good to us unless You're at full strength." Niki gave me that "look" that let me know she wasn't only talking about work. "We have people on this, and we'll be able to track this guy down, now that he's out in the open with his identity. The other issue can wait until You get better."

There were times when having two submissive women at your beck and call could be considered a good thing for the average man. This was not one of those times. I tried not to seethe over the fact that they were keeping me from doing what needed to be done, and in my mind, there was no one else who could do the job right.

The minute I tried to get up and Natasha was able to ease me back in place without breaking much of a sweat let me know that my mind was writing checks that my body couldn't cash right now. I slammed my head against the pillows, cursing out no one in particular but wanting to find a target or two. "Fine, you have twenty-four hours. The moment the doctors release Me, I'm going to be in South Georgia to handle some shit and get the answers that I need. Are we clear?"

"Crystal clear, my Sir." Natasha tried not to grin, but I knew I'd triggered one of her fetishes. She loved it when I was aggressive with my words and actions. It didn't work on Niki so much; she was more of an action junkie. She lifted my hand to kiss the back of my palm before kissing my cheek. "Now, if You'll excuse me, i have a suspect to try and track down."

"Yes, and i have a bit of political maneuvering that i have to do to get through this debacle of a case with the Ashton kidnapping." Niki followed her sister's lead, kissing my palm before kissing my cheek and making her way out the door also. That left Ramesses and me in the room alone, with nothing more than a long-overdue chat about the cases to work through.

I took my phone and texted Ty. I needed some dirt to bring with me when I confronted Sarge. I told him to come clean so I could protect him, but he decided it was best to act like I couldn't touch him. The leverage he used to have over me didn't even apply anymore; the minute I quit the department, the ability to have me prosecuted went out the window.

I didn't think he was aware of that, but I didn't care anymore. Lives were at stake.

Ramesses gave me a look, almost like he was disappointed that I'd found myself in such a predicament. He stroked his beard, trying to figure out how he wanted to approach the conversation between us. I returned his stare with a dismissive glance of my own, letting him know that I had already plotted some get back, whether he approved of it or not.

"You know You should have gotten grimy and killed that dude, right?"

"I thought I was getting grimy. Turned out, he was a little hungrier than I was."

"Sometimes You gotta lose a few to figure out how to get the W."

I wasn't interested in hearing the metaphorical psych job he was imparting on me, no matter how much I might have needed to hear it. The next time I saw him, I wouldn't take him for granted;

I knew who I was dealing with, and this next time, I would not make the same mistakes. "Yeah, yeah, spare me the speeches and rhetoric, Sir. The fact that he got the drop on Me has Me in payback mode. Being stuck in here isn't helping matters, either; I need to be on the streets. I'm not about to sit here and do nothing."

"You don't have a choice in the matter, Your body is telling You that right now. Be patient, get stronger, and execute the plan that's in Your head."

"That plan got formed the minute I woke up in here. He has no idea what I'm about to do to him, and he won't see it coming this time."

"So, what are You gonna do when You get out of here?"

"I'm gonna find him, and I'm gonna send him back to his Mistress."

"Bold words, partner. You sure You can back them up in Your condition?"

"Watch Me."

TWENTY-ONE

"*Hi, baby, have you missed me?*"

"*Wait a minute…Sherrie? How are you here? How is this possible?*"

"*You called for me in the darkness, baby, so, here I am.*"

"*But you're dead. This can't be real; why are you here, baby?*"

"*Because you're having problems solving these cases, and you called out for me.*"

It had to be the sedative that the nurses gave me to help me sleep; there was no other way to explain what was happening to me. I was hallucinating, or something, but the way she looked, the way she felt—or at least in my mind it felt like she was right there—it almost seemed real.

However it happened, it was a bittersweet mixture of happiness and anxiety. I took comfort that I could call out for her and my mind could trick me into thinking she was actually there with me, but I felt a bit selfish, thinking I could somehow find the peace that I couldn't find before she died.

"*You always knew when I was having trouble cracking cases, Sherrie. I miss that about you, about us.*"

"*Yes, but you have two women in your life now who can fill that void for you.*"

"*Yeah, but I'm stuck in this room until they release me. I can't be any good to anyone laid up like this.*"

"*Dom, baby, listen to me; you'll be fine, you've handled cases tougher than this, including my case. I have faith that you will be able to do what is necessary in the end."*

She was right; I was stressing out over cases that didn't hold a candle to the ones that had a higher degree of difficulty. I was pressing more than I should have, and I knew the reason why; I simply didn't want to admit it to myself. I couldn't believe that I allowed someone to have that much power over my psyche, but I did, and I needed to find a way to break her hold over me.

"You know you can't trust Simone; she's proven herself to be a bit psychotic, especially after killing me over some perceived slight she had against us. Do you think for one moment that she won't flip on you and try to get a reduced sentence out of it?"

"She won't get away with whatever she thinks she's getting away with, baby. She knows if she crosses me that it means big problems for her."

"Like what, more time in prison? That's not going to faze her one bit." Her voice felt like it was trying to draw me in, make me a part of her world. Her words were soothing, with a hint of edginess to make me feel like I was alive. *"Please make sure that you bury her deeper once you've found out the truth behind her supposedly helping you in this case, D. I don't think you realize how deep her problems with you run. She's always been fixated on you; even in college it was on the border-line of creepy. She lives to see you squirm, my love. Don't let her think she has the upper hand."*

"But, how do I get her to crack, baby? She's always tried to stay two steps ahead of me."

"Dominic, she's always tried to make you believe that, but I know my man better than that." She was convinced of everything she was saying to me, and it gave me the most serene feeling. I couldn't believe I was hearing these things, but my mind went back to the woman in the hotel, the one who told me that Sherrie was having second thoughts about us before she was killed. *"You were always*

the best at what you did, and you still are. Look past the false arrogance that makes her think she's better or smarter than you, and you'll have what you need to make her crack and tell you everything you need to know. I believe in you, baby; I always have, and I always will."

"I love you, Sherrie. I never stopped loving you." The tears I felt while inside of my hallucinogenic dream as they made their way down my cheeks were real, and my emotions were high. I felt the need to say what I wanted to say while I felt I had her attention, whether it was real or imagined. "*I wish there was a way to have saved you before she killed you.*"

"*We'll be together again, my love. In the next life, we'll get it right, and no one will stand in our way. Until then, make the best of this life, and do what you were born to do. Now, get up and take care of business. I'll be watching over you, always, until the time comes for us to be together again.*"

Leave it to Sherrie to know how to help me when I least expected it. I really wished I wasn't on the powerful narcotics that I was under, but I had a feeling that it wouldn't take long before things would get back to normal. Even in death, she still had a profound effect on me, and I'd love her forever for that.

And even in my dream state, my ex-wife gave me what I needed to gain the advantage over Simone.

"How are you holding up, bruh?"

I still had a protective brace over my bruised ribs as I walked up the hallway to check on Ty. He had gotten beat up pretty bad, and I'd hoped that he made it out of his condo in one piece. I was still unconscious when the paramedics had gotten to me, according to what I was told, and despite my questions about him, in my diminished state, I probably wouldn't have heard that he made it through and was going to be okay.

Ty gave a weak smile, trying to get through his own pains as he gave me the once-over.

"Obviously, not as well as you are, man. Already on your feet in less than a day? I need to figure out how you heal so quickly so I can be like you. This hospital food is fucking with my normal diet."

"I wish I could come up with the formula for you, but you know me, I'm part stubborn as hell, too." I put up a good front for him, but if I was honest, I should have kept my ass in bed and taken it easy. "How in the world did he get past your system?"

Ty shook his head, realizing that he had to explain the whole ordeal. "He caught me slipping while I was coming out of Lenox Square. He followed me home, and in hindsight I should have seen him coming a mile away, but I was on the phone with this girl and she was trying to swing by, and that was a wrap."

"So, he forced you into the house?"

"Yeah, he came at me fast and hard, hit me and dropped me on the ground. He dragged me inside, trying to find out what I knew about him, what I'd dug up on him. When I told him that I didn't know who the fuck he was, he swore I was lying and tried to beat the information out of me." Ty continued to recount what he could remember. "My phone went off while he was punching me, and he saw your name pop up, so that's when he told me to call you and get you to come over, or he would kill me."

If I didn't want to put this guy in the ground before, I was absolutely focused on making sure that happened now. I no longer cared about whether he went to prison for his crimes; my only concern was making him suffer for what he had managed to try to do, and in Jason's and Tori's cases, what he already did.

"Listen, I need you to heal up as best you can. I have the information you were able to dig up to help me take care of things and find the bastard. You have my word I'll make him pay for what he's done."

"Bruh, you know I already know what you plan to do. That son of a bitch tried to kill me and he already killed two people who were close to you. You don't need my permission, and you certainly don't owe me anything. We've been friends too long for all of that." Ty raised his arm to tap fists with mine, a smile spreading across his face as one of the nurses walked in to do her check. The smirk on her face let me know he'd been working on her ever since he got in here. "Besides, if I hadn't had what happened to me happen, I wouldn't have met Valencia. So, in a really warped way, I should thank you for getting me put in here. She's been worth going through the pain while she helps me get better."

Yeah, he needed help to get better, all right. The shape on Valencia made it worth staying in here at least another week, just to make sure that the wounds healed properly.

I headed out the door to prepare to get discharged. "Don't hurt yourself too bad while you're recuperating, bruh. I'm sure you want to get back to what you do best soon. And I'm sure Valencia won't mind administering private home care once you leave."

"You got that right." Ty continued to admire the international flavor that had his attention. "Can you do me a favor, though? When you catch ol' boy, don't bother making him suffer. Put him out of his misery."

TWENTY-TWO

I walked through the door of the prison like a man possessed.

I wasn't alone, either; by the looks of the faces of the people watching as I moved through the building, they'd have thought I was of some importance. I wasn't, but that's none of their business.

I made the phone call to have Sarge meet us in the reception area of the building as soon as possible. It was my final heads-up and courtesy to him, and a rather ironic one at that. He was a good man, at least in my eyes, but his arrogance did him in. It wasn't something I would take pleasure in, but there was no other choice in the matter anymore. It was up to me to show him the error of his ways, whether he wanted me to or not.

The unfortunate part of all of this was that there was only one way that this was going to end. I couldn't do this alone, and I recognized that, which is why I made the connections I did to make this all happen. If I was going to have a high-ranking member of the Department of Corrections removed from his position, I had to have a few people who had more clout than he did.

"Are you certain about these allegations, Detective Law?" one of the persons walking with me asked. "He's been one of our more distinguished employees, despite the issues he had before leaving Fulton County PD."

"Ms. Altmore, I wouldn't have asked you to accompany me down here if I wasn't absolutely certain about the allegations I'm levying against him." The recording was compelling, but it wasn't quite enough to bring formal charges against him, that much I was already aware of. I had to put him on the spot, whether he liked it or not. "I realize he is one of your more valued employees, which makes this especially hard to deal with. I was one of his former subordinates; I realize the difficulties I'm dealing with."

There's always been this thing about the "thin, blue line" that we're supposed to never cross, but to be honest, I'd never really subscribed to that theory. Yes, I had no issues sticking up for my brothers in blue if the situation called for that to occur, but if there was some issue, or it looked like there was something shady going on, I was not going to look the other way. It didn't endear me to a lot of officers during my years in various precincts, although it did put me squarely in the crosshairs of Internal Affairs for recruitment purposes. In hindsight, it might be the root cause of why I had been catching so much flak from former coworkers and current officers whenever I came into contact.

It might have also explained why Sarge was so flippant in his concern for what I was capable of doing to him professionally. In his mind, no one would back me up since I wasn't exactly ever one of them, and now that I was in the private sector, that reality was even more pronounced. If I was honest with myself, I had to look in the mirror to find the blame for all the friction I continued to encounter. Whether or not I would be able to change that perception would be a matter of time and consistency.

That also had everything to do with the entourage walking with me, too.

The other people that were in the group making its way to Sarge's office were the attorneys who represented the Legal Services division, along with two officers who were there for detainment purposes, should the attorneys deem a necessity for such an action to occur. That explained the way everyone moved out of the way or tried to stay busy to keep from drawing attention to themselves. This was the extraction group, and whomever they were coming to extract, they made sure they did everything they could to not be the focus of the extraction.

This was the first phase of my plan; the next phase required the presence of the defense attorney who represented Simone. His presence was necessary so he could witness the testimony of his client and advise her of her rights, which as a prisoner, she truly didn't have very many. Combine what she knew in one instance with the information that could help me place a dangerous man behind bars, and she had no choice but to cooperate. The other choice was life in a super-max prison, relocated out of Georgia, where she wouldn't be able to harm anyone else again.

I wasn't stupid; I might have been prepared to perform one hellish interrogation, but the criminal law degree hanging in my office compelled me to make sure this would be as righteous a maneuver as it needed to be. Before I was done with her, two things were going to happen: the first thing was that she would give me everything, every piece of information she was privy to, including the person who put this whole mess together; the second thing was that her attorney would have no choice but to advise her that she would give me everything, especially when she committed a murder while incarcerated.

Even when she did give me everything, she was still going to get upgraded and relocated. She's a high-risk prisoner now, and those would have to be dealt with in a different manner altogether.

Look, I never said this would have a happy ending for her; I only said everything I was doing would result in a righteous arrest and conviction.

She could wait, though; I had a bigger fish to catch and kill.

Sarge had already been summoned to the reception area, and he didn't look pleased about it at all. The expression on his face and the look he gave me could have melted lead. "I see you decided to try to bury me after all, huh? Well, I won't go down alone, that's for fucking sure."

"Now, now, there's no need for that type of language, especially around the ladies, sir." I did my best to maintain some decorum while dealing with the delicate nature of this meeting. He was willing to drudge up my past transgressions, and I was ready for every one of them. "There's also no need to drag this out any longer than it has to; these people are here because I have leveled some serious charges against you."

"Yes, I read the list; you're stretching, Law. That's disappointing, too; I thought I taught you better than that." Sarge was insistent on trying to push my buttons to get me to crack, but what he forgot was that we were both seasoned veterans, and I was no longer one of his subordinates. "What proof do you have that I did any of what you're alleging me of doing?"

"I believe that might be where I come in." Simone walked up with an armed guard on her heels, shackled from wrist to ankle in chains and cuffs. "Considering I know I'm not going anywhere anytime soon, I would say I have information that might put you in a rather negative light, Assistant Warden Lynch."

His eyes narrowed upon seeing Simone, and even more irritated once her attorney stood by her side. He couldn't stop laughing, almost like the joke was on us. "You really have got to be kidding me right now. You're going to believe the word of a junkie convict over me?"

"I think you have me mixed up with some of the other inmates you've been fucking the past few months, dude." Simone smirked, dropping some information that even I wasn't aware of. The shocked expression on Sarge's face was enough to lend credibility to her impromptu claims. "Yeah, the thing you did to set that girl up in my cell is the least of your problems, I would think."

"This bitch is lying on some major league levels! I want my attorney here, now!" Sarge bellowed, causing the officers to take a flanking stance. He scoffed at them, almost like he was insulted that they were trying to detain him. "She has nothing on me, period. It's her word against mine, and I promise you it won't hold up in court."

"I guess it depends on the information that she has in her possession that might incriminate you, Warden Lynch." I looked at Ms. Altmore, and I wasn't sure if things would get better or worse than this moving forward, but one thing was for sure; it was about to get entertaining quickly. "I guess we'll have to see what happens in court to know the final answer on that, Sarge. Now, if you would allow these gentlemen to escort you off the premises, it will help move things along smoothly."

"Let me tell you a story, and I think you're gonna love how this one turns out, Dom."

Simone had all but ignored her attorney's advice to shut up and not say anything, even as the Legal Services attorneys pretty much said the same thing to her. For some reason, she felt the need to stick it to me one last time. I guess she needed to get her sadistic rocks off and purge her soul at the same time, but I wasn't exactly in the mood for her smug attitude. I had aces in the hole that she knew nothing about, thanks to some unexpected information that was texted to me by Ty from his hospital bed.

If she wanted to play high-stakes poker with her life, I was more than willing to oblige her.

"So, tell me, Simone, how am I going to enjoy how this story turns out, huh? It's bad enough you hid a murder from me; what other well-kept secrets do you think you have that you might enjoy torturing me with?" I didn't mind the games this time around; I wanted to see how much information she was willing to tell me of her own volition. "I'm sure we all would love to hear about this."

"You're a little fuller of yourself than usual, D. You must think you know something that I don't."

I played the first weak card in my hand, to see if she'd bite. "I might have something up my sleeve, Simone. Maybe I should start with the fact that I know Kacie was your cellmate. Does that open you up a little bit?"

A slow clap came from her hands as she cocked her head to the side to acknowledge my response. "Well, damn, I guess you're not all brawn after all. Yes, D, she was my cellmate, so what of it? Oh, let me guess, you think I murdered her, don't you?"

"I don't think, Simone; I know you did." I followed up my weak card with a stronger card to make her sweat a little bit. "According to the assistant warden, she was found in your cell, her neck broken, and it happened after bed check that night. There was no one else in the cell or around the cell at the estimated time of the murder, and your cells are under camera surveillance. Care to explain?"

I watched her face turn desperate in a second, almost like she wanted to beat Sarge to the punch when it came to turning state's evidence. "She was planted in my cell, and the bitch decided she wanted the top bunk, like she was supposed to be some special bitch or something. One night in particular, she called herself saying she had special permission or some shit, and she'd only been here for a freaking week."

I leaned back in the chair across from her, watching the proverbial noose lowering around her neck. She was playing into my hands and she was smiling all the way.

"About another week into it, Lynch comes to me during my work detail and he has this proposition for me, saying he would be able to make things easier for me after I did this thing for him." Simone tried to gauge my facial expressions, realizing that I was all into every word she was saying. That's what I wanted her to think. "Then, I get this guest out of the blue that wants to talk to me. At first, I didn't know what to trust, but as the conversation continued during that first meeting, I began to see the bigger picture, and I was down for the cause immediately."

"Wait a minute; what guest are you talking about? Who came to see you?"

"Let's just say, we had a mutual problem that needed to be taken care of." She grinned at me, springing the trap I wanted her to fall into. "In exchange for my services, Lynch would get me into minimum security and a better work detail, and I could serve my sentence in peace and tranquility."

I almost felt sorry for her. She had no idea that Sarge had already confessed to his part in the conspiracy and was summarily being arrested and charged as such. He even gave up the information as to where the money came from that he was paid to pull this whole thing off. The only thing he didn't give up was the person who financed this situation, which apparently was aimed at getting back at me for something else I must have done to them in a former life.

I would soon realize how accurate I actually was.

I kept listening to her ramblings as I continued to take notes. There was still one other last bit of information that I needed to close the loophole and really get into hunting mode: who was the person that set all of this in motion?

"So, basically you killed Kacie, but what I'm not understanding is why? Outside of the perks, what the fuck was really in it for you? Or were you manipulated into thinking that you were getting some sick joy out of watching me squirm?" I was getting impatient, although I didn't exactly show it. I was already weary of her long-winded tactics and nearly had half a mind to go back to Sarge and press him for the name so I could go back to Atlanta and finish this once and for all.

Simone looked as exasperated as I was. "Look, my life is done already, all right? I'm not getting out of here anyway; I'll be serving life now, thanks to the fucking murder I committed, so what the fuck does it matter if I take the mystery out of things and let you deal with the consequences?"

"Well, then, put me out of my misery, Simone. Tell me what the hell is going on."

"The person who had been visiting me was a woman. She looked about as slick and slimy as a politician, and she talked that way, too. She came at me with this thing; told me that Lynch was in on it." Simone took a breath to work through her thoughts. "She said that you fucked her life up and she wanted revenge for what you took from her. She didn't want it to be an easy mark, so that's how Karrion got brought into the mix."

The more she talked, the more she tripped different memories I had over the events of the past year. The players came into clearer focus, and I almost wanted to shout to the high heavens once I realized another ghost from my past—this time, my recent past—was hell-bent on taking me out.

I remembered Karrion from a little over a year ago, during Kacie's sentencing phase of her trial. He begged the court to be lenient, that he couldn't live without her and that she wasn't a bad person. But that wasn't the man that I dealt with and nearly got killed fighting. Once my mind began to process that day at the trial again as she rambled, I recognized his facial features. They were a little more chiseled and harder-edged than the softer submissive that I remembered in that courtroom.

He must have put on a lot of weight and muscle while she was in prison. I wasn't sure if that was a good thing or a bad thing; the way he fought me, he resembled a rabid dog who couldn't be stopped, but he could be controlled. The way I saw it, he was being controlled by someone else, especially when Kacie was now dead.

He was convinced by someone that I, and everyone around me, was directly responsible for the death of his Domina, and that person also convinced him that they had a shared plight, and that together, they could make us all pay for taking her away from him. At the same time, the long-sought revenge would come full circle.

"We've been planning this for months, Dom, and she's been behind the scenes, pulling all the strings." She cackled with her laughter, which only sent chills up my spine. "She said you would be late to the party, trying to focus more on the case than the underlying layers that still pointed back toward you. I wasn't shocked, though; you picked up on everything a lot quicker than she said you would. I half expected everyone around you to be dead before you figured it all out. Bravo, bravo."

The more she talked, the more clues she gave up. *She's been behind the scenes…she's been pulling all the strings.*

I wanted to curse as loudly as I could. I really played myself by thinking that she would have left well enough alone and lived happily ever after with her congressman husband. Something must have happened to change the game so drastically to where she needed to come for me like this. If I were to guess, it might have had something to do with the six-figure payment I guessed she wasn't able to explain away when it disappeared from their accounts.

Veronica *fucking* Emerson.

Simone stopped in the midst of her monologue to recognize my revelation. "Well, I'll be damned, he figured that out, too. So, how does it feel to fuck over another woman, Dom? I honestly don't feel so bad now; for a while, I thought I was the only one. It's nice to have some company for a change."

"Yeah, you're about to have company, all right. I'm going to see to it that you two are cellmates for the next few decades." The anger in my body was really about to boil over, and I was hours away from where I needed to be to quell that anger. "You just couldn't leave well enough alone, could you?"

"Please, spare me the outrage. You didn't have a problem letting me rot in here for the next ten-to-twenty. Now, thanks to you, I won't ever see the light of day. All you had to do was tell the damn judge that I was worthy of a lighter sentence." I knew what she wanted, but I wasn't about to give it to her, either. Dragging out an old argument didn't do anyone any good, and it was going to do nothing but waste more time. "You still couldn't see past your own selfishness, and look where it's gotten you. If you're not careful, you're going to end up burying someone else who's close to you."

My cell phone rang as she continued to rant, and I stepped away from her to answer it. "Law."

"It seems we have some unfinished business, you and me."

I gritted my teeth so hard I felt like I was going to need caps before too long. "How the fuck did you get my number?"

"Dom! We're outside of the—" I heard Natasha's voice screaming over his earpiece before I heard a smack and then an uncomfortable silence. I heard another woman's voice, but I couldn't make it out before he pulled the phone away.

"Well, that was unfortunate." Karrion's calm tone worried me more than I wanted to admit to. Usually when people were calm like that, they already had the plan mapped out in their head as to what they were going to do next. "So, now that I have your attention, I think it's time you and I finished this, don't you agree?"

Simone was yelling in the background, obviously pissed that I'd ignored her completely. "Dom, get back over here, dammit! We're not done talking yet! Dom! DOM!"

I really didn't give a fuck about her anymore; she'd given me what I wanted and there was no more use for her. There was nothing else left for her to say, and I wasn't worried about a reprisal from her anymore, either. By this time next week, she would be in a maximum-security location where they only let prisoners out for an hour a day to keep them from going completely insane.

If I was a lesser man, I'd have someone take her out. Hell, it would be considered an act of mercy, as far as I was concerned. She no longer served a purpose on this earth, and this would mark the second time that she had been responsible for the death of someone close to me.

If anything happened to Natasha, she was going to beg me to kill her to keep from suffering the torture I would have planned for her. I was done being the nice guy. What worried me more was the other woman whose voice I heard when Natasha tried to tell me where she was. That made matters worse.

"Tell me who you have first, and then I'll let you know if you think you can get on my level to finish whatever business you think we have."

The next thing I heard was the panicked screams of sajira's voice sounding off in my ears. Karrion pulled the phone away once again, this time his voice giving off a bit more urgency to his repeated question. "So, are you ready to finish this, or do you need more convincing?"

The only thing that mattered now was finding Karrion and erasing him from the map. He might not have realized what he'd started, but he was about to find out how pissed off he'd made me. "Name the place and time, bitch, and I'll make sure to show up so I can personally punch your boarding pass to the hereafter."

"Not if I don't send you there first, overnight express shipping."

"Stop flapping your gums and tell me where you are. I think you're as tired of playing these hide-and-seek games as I am. If you think you're ready, show me if you're about that life, because I don't think you are."

He was really testing the limits of my patience. There was some silence on the phone before he spoke again, and this time, there was no hesitation in his cadence. "If you think I'm going to make it that easy for you, you're dumber than you look. But when you do figure it out, make sure you come alone, or your bitch and her friend will be awaiting you in hell."

TWENTY-THREE

"Are you sure that's where she is? Dom, I need you to think this through."

Niki tried to sound like the voice of reason as I got into the city just before nightfall. I was relieved that I made it under the cover of darkness; it served as the perfect backdrop for the massacre that was about to ensue.

Ty tried to pick up on the "find my iPhone" app that was on Natasha's phone to give me an idea of where she was, but to no avail. He mentioned that her phone was turned off, only revealing the last location before the phone no longer transmitted.

He heard the tension in my voice and had the same words for me to try and think before I reacted, but there was no way for me to do that. All that mattered to me was finding my girl and sajira in one piece and finding Karrion before leaving him in a heap of broken pieces.

Ramesses was beside himself, yelling at the detail that was supposed to keep sajira in their sight. The response felt like something out of a scene from *Mission: Impossible*: they were taken out by someone with tranquilizer darts and took sajira in seconds. They never had a chance.

Ty tried his best to keep the both of us from going off half-cocked into a situation that we weren't equipped to handle. This was becoming more problematic than I originally intended. I needed backup if I was going to get out of this alive.

"Listen, unless we have another way to find them, this is going to feel like finding a needle in a virtual haystack." Ty rubbed his hands over his face in frustration, unsure of what he could do to alleviate the stress of the situation. "I mean, tech can only go so far as long as it's functional and powered. Even the locator apps can go but so far."

Ramesses snapped his fingers. "Ty, pull up the radar from my office. I think I have the needle you're looking for."

I forgot about the tracking chips! Karrion was going to be in for the shock of his life!

A couple of clicks later, and sajira's sensor popped up on the screen. Pin-point accuracy to the damn room in the house where they were being held.

I couldn't get out of the office fast enough!

"Listen, D, I need you to make sure that you know what you're doing, okay? If what Simone said was true, then Veronica might have a few people in your way before you even get to Karrion." He might have been right about that, but I had a few tricks up my sleeve, too. Karrion might have said come alone, but he was working off the premise that I was hoping he would do the same thing.

By the time I got to the address that was given to me, it was a pretty damn good guess that not only was Karrion not alone, but from the information on the owner of the house, I would be able to kill two birds with one stone.

This was starting to play out like some weird drama, and I wasn't about to be the Pyrrhic hero, either. The way I saw it, if I planned this right, there should be minimal casualties and that should be about it. One wrong move and I'd lose more than what I bargained for.

My cell phone rang before I hit the gate, and I picked it up without a care of who it was. "Law."

"Sir, where is my sis? I need to know where to send units so You don't have to do this." Niki's voice sang through my earpiece, but the sing-song I was used to was replaced by cold-as-ice professionalism. "You're not one hundred percent, my Sir. i don't want anything to happen to You or Natasha."

"I can't tell you where they are, Niki."

"They?"

"He had someone grab sajira, too. I assume for added insurance."

"Oh my God. Sir, You're going to need backup—"

"Trust Me, baby girl, I have backup. Everything is under control, and I promise I'll bring them both back alive. I'll call you once it's over."

Niki's pleas to tell her where Natasha was continued to go unanswered, eventually meeting the dead air of a disconnected phone call. I couldn't risk the chance of her bringing the boys yet, not until I was able to take care of business. I also couldn't risk Karrion following through on the threat to kill the girls if he had a hint of law enforcement being in the area.

I had to do this off the grid; there was no other choice in the matter.

He was expecting to see me alone, and that's exactly what he was going to get.

At least, that's what I was going to make him believe he was going to get.

🔫🔫🔫

I drove to the front gate, waiting for the security guard to open it. Well, actually, I wasn't exactly waiting, so to speak. I only needed the guard to see my car long enough to open the gate and come through, which wouldn't have tripped the alarm system, for starters, and he wouldn't have had a chance to warn the other guards near the house.

One quick squeeze of the trigger from the eyes lurking in the shadows made quick work of him.

One moment, he was trying to figure out why I was on the grounds. The next moment, he was on the ground, never to rise again, his carotid artery pierced deep enough to have him bleed out in seconds.

Once inside, I drove to the front of the house, parking my car in the driveway before getting out of the car. I tapped my ear for a minute before I headed for the front door, meeting one of Veronica's bodyguards before I even got to knock.

Seconds later, he felt a sting right around the lapel of his coat.

A few seconds after that, he was a heap on the ground as the wound began to seep, staining his coat and the shirt underneath.

"One down, D. Got about seven more to go on the inside." I heard V12's voice loud and clear in my earpiece, letting me know my Guardian Angel would be on my shoulder the entire way. "I see two on the stairs. You take one, I got the other one."

"Bet."

I pulled one of my guns out, screwing the silencer on as soon as I had the chance to move. The less noise I could make, the better the chances were I could get Natasha and sajira out alive.

I saw the first gunman at the top of the stairs before he saw me. Before he could pull his gun, I already had the sights trained on his neck. A quick squeeze of the trigger and he went down easy, sounding like a sack of potatoes hitting the ground.

The second guard came running to find out what happened to his buddy. He got hit in mid-stride, with the only sound I heard was glass cracking from the bullet coming through the window from V12's vantage point. "Three more in the hallway, near the bedroom, D. I see your girl and Ramesses's girl and another female in there, but I don't see the mark."

"I got you, bruh. I have a feeling he's in the cut, waiting for me to find him again." I was not about to go for the bullshit again. "Check your scope near the bedroom; there's gotta be a heat signature close by."

I pulled close to the bedroom door, noticing the other three that my sniper saw through the heat scopes. I threw a flash grenade, no longer worrying about noise in the immense estate, waiting for the men to react to it before I started firing again.

Their screams were enough to draw Karrion out from his hiding place, but before I could get to him, he slipped inside the bedroom door. He had the advantage, at least for the moment, as V12 made quick work of the other men still reeling from the effects of the grenade. "He's all yours, D. Happy hunting."

I opened the door to the bedroom, waiting a few seconds before entering inside, and to my surprise, Karrion was standing in the middle of the room with this slick grin on his face. Now that I had a chance to get a look at him, I slowly understood how he was able to get the drop on me and overpower me when I was at Ty's. He was a lot bigger, more muscular, than I'd counted on from my memory.

I still could take him in a straight-up brawl, but my body wasn't completely healed from our last encounter, and trying to engage like that would be a fool's mission. I had hoped to be able to appeal to his rational mind, but there were two problems with that plan, and one of them didn't look at all happy to see me.

Veronica sat in the room with him, and Natasha and sajira were on the bed not far from where Veronica was sitting. In Veronica's hand was a small .22-caliber handgun; not tremendously large or powerful, but it was enough to get the job done if it was aimed at the right area. "I really didn't think you would be stupid enough to really show up by yourself like that, but considering my guards are presumed dead, I think I underestimated you, Law."

"Yeah, I'm just full of surprises tonight, huh?"

"I think you might want to put the gun down, cuteness. I'd hate to be the one to take your girl out after you came all this way to make sure she didn't die. Hell, I wonder what your partner would say if he found out you caused his girl to die, too." Her eyes were wild, looking in Natasha's direction as she pulled the slider back to load a bullet in the chamber. Her eyes darted toward sajira before she spoke again. "Do you want to take the chance that I'm a bad shot, Dom?

I don't think you want to."

I closed my eyes for a minute as I heard V12 in my ear. "You don't have to take him, D; your body is not up for it. You just got out the hospital yesterday. Two shots and it's over with."

What he was saying wasn't the complete truth, but it wasn't a total lie, either. If I tried to get with Karrion head-up, there was a distinct possibility I was going to lose more than just the fight. I opened my eyes and looked over at Natasha, watching her eyes as she shook her head, silently echoing the sentiments of the voice in my ear, despite the fact that she couldn't have possibly heard what he was telling me. sajira echoed the sentiments, her eyes pleading me to end this some other way than some showdown that I might end up losing.

V12 was still in my ear, giving me options that might have made this clean and easy. "Say the word, and I'll slice through her hand to take the gun out of the play. Next shot and I can take out her pet."

Karrion seemed to think he was involved with whatever was about to go down. He tried the punk move first to see if he could rattle my cage. "Aww, come on, Dom? I know you've been dying to get some payback from me putting you in the hospital. Come on, I know you want some; come get some!"

I never took my hands off my gun, but I did lower it for a moment to figure out my options. With V12 still in my ear, imploring me to take the shot so he could disarm Veronica, I found myself wondering if I really could take him, even in my weakened condition. The indecision felt foreign to me; under normal circumstances, I would have simply told Karrion I was dropping the gun and the dance would begin immediately. Veronica would get the show she wanted, but the only problem I faced was that I was in a no-win situation.

If I killed Karrion, Veronica had me in her sights and she would probably take me out in a heartbeat. If I didn't kill Karrion, he was going to finish off. Now that his handler was there to give the order, there would be nothing to stop him, except for V12 taking him out, which would set off a chain of events that would end in the murders of Natasha and sajira.

That I couldn't allow.

"Say the word, D, I got you." V12 was getting antsy, and I couldn't blame him, but I had to see if there was a way to talk them both down and find a more sane and peaceful solution. "I can take them both with two shots; you don't have to drag this out."

I looked over at Veronica, my gun still lowered, and I tried to see if I could get to the woman that lay underneath the crazy that I witnessed on the surface. "Veronica, you don't have to do this. I'm sure whatever it was that you think I'm responsible for, it's all in your head, okay? You have this man thinking that we killed his Mistress, when you were the one who had her killed in prison."

Karrion heard that information and immediately turned to Veronica, looking for answers. "Is this true? Did you have my Mistress killed? Tell me that can't be true!"

Veronica's eyes widened, as she didn't think I had that information at my disposal. She wanted to shake her head to tell Karrion not to believe me, but her silence betrayed her badly. When she finally spoke, I noticed that her hold on Karrion wasn't as strong as it was before. "Sweetie, you know he's lying to get you to turn against me. You can't believe a word he's saying. He's a PI; they're paid to twist the truth."

Karrion seemed more interested in the non-answer than he was the other spins and rhetoric that came from her lips. "I don't think I heard a yes or a no in response to my question, so I'm going to ask you one more time; did you have my Mistress killed?"

He began to move in her direction, wanting to hear the answer from her lips, the sneer present on his lips. He moved closer to her, his eyes trained on her face, waiting for her to answer. "Well, are you going to tell me or not?"

Veronica lifted her arm and squeezed the trigger in one motion, hitting Karrion between his eyes. As his body dropped to the floor, she finally opened her mouth to verbalize, knowing he would never hear the answer. "Yes, you weak-ass bitch, I killed her. Happy now?"

As I watched his body drop, my emotions were all over the place. I wanted to be the one to take him out, but I was relieved that I didn't have to worry about taking on a man who was in "Hulk Smash!" mode and probably had the damn adrenaline to keep up with the mentality.

The other thing was the cold-blooded nature of how Veronica simply shot him. The fact that she didn't hesitate let me know that this thing was far from over, and despite no one to back her up, that made things more precarious, if anything. I kept my gun drawn, never taking her out of my sight. Her eyes were still wild, daring me to figure out if I was willing to take her out or if I was going to be a cop and take her into custody.

My attempt to engage in a dialog was my only way out of this, so I appealed to her vanity and superiority. "Beauty and brains, huh? You had me scrambling from the first day, Veronica. What did you have in mind for the finale?"

"You just had to put me in the position to kill him, didn't you?" Veronica's body language was completely closed off, leaving no way for me to talk her down from the ledge she was dead-set on jumping from. Her eyes never left mine as she kept the finger on the trigger. "No matter where I turn, you're always there, fucking up my plans. I had a nice racket going out in Dallas, and then you had to go and screw that up. Then, after triggering that damn clause and payment, my husband divorced me, picking up a newer modeled trophy wife. Do you know what he said to me after the divorce?"

"Veronica, I'm—"

"Shut the fuck up! You're going to listen to every goddamned word I have to say before I kill you." She was at the point of no return, and I needed to make sure I didn't miss when the time came to shoot. She raised the gun, her hands shaking this time as her anger and emotions began to take over from her logical mind. "He was so cold about it, like I'd taken one of his children or something. He basically said he should have gotten rid of me years ago because I forgot how to stay in my lane and be the trophy wife that he needed to keep his career going. Dropped me for one of his pretty little interns he was fucking at the office."

I started to say something to break her from her extended monologue, but the barrel was trained on me. I couldn't take the chance of her having a moment, so I kept my mouth shut.

"Then, when I tried to make a play for you, and you turned me down, I started wondering if he had a point. Maybe I was being a bit too much that even run-of-the-mill dudes on the street didn't want to bother with me. I was a congressman's wife, dammit! I don't deal with dudes that ain't on my level!"

She's unstable; the divorce did her in. It probably didn't help that she might not have had a leg to stand on if they had a prenuptial agreement, and she got so comfortable being in the lap of luxury with a man who got kickbacks—well, allegedly speaking—that she didn't bother making her own money or at least kept something on the side for such emergencies.

I had to check my proverbial pockets to see if I could find any fucks to give about her life post-cushy-ass-marriage, and when I couldn't find any, I basically looked for the trigger that would set this off. With V12 in my ear, I silently gave the green light to take the shot when he was ready.

"You know what, there's nothing wrong with dudes who ain't on your level, seriously." I began to bait her, more to take her eyes off Natasha and sajira than anything else. I didn't want her trying anything stupid. "What you should have been doing this entire time, instead of focusing on me, you should have taken the money that you tried to pay Sarge off and done what you needed to do to get back on track. He paid you off; I know he did. But no, you had to come after someone who really wasn't thinking anything about you."

I heard sirens faintly blaring in the distance. I figured someone heard the flash grenade and called the police to check things out. I had no choice but to speed this up, or it could turn into a hostage situation, and I didn't need that. It almost never ended well for the shooter.

"Well, you won't be thinking about much of anything anymore, especially once I cancel your bitch." Veronica turned toward Natasha and made the motion to shoot.

Instincts took over; I had to act fast. I squeezed the trigger, aiming for her shoulder to take her down. She took the hit, but somehow she only stepped back a few paces, moving toward Natasha like she was possessed. She fired off a shot, aiming for Natasha but barely missing sajira, still moving toward them to get a closer shot. I didn't want to kill her, trying to get her to think about what she was doing before she would regret it.

"I don't want to kill you, Veronica!"

"You're going to have to kill me, Dom! I'll kill her if you don't kill me!"

The sirens got louder; it was only a matter of time before they arrived at the house. I told V12 to clear out of the area and I'd take the blame for the aftermath. He all but ignored the order, telling me that he was not leaving me until this was over. He didn't leave me much choice, but I also knew that if anyone in the Squad could get out of a tight spot, it was definitely him.

I watched Veronica as she continued to walk toward Natasha and sajira, ignoring my orders to stop. I realized there was no other choice and I was going to have to take her out.

I pulled my other weapon, squeezing the trigger once more, watching her body drop in mid-step, going for the shot that would put her out of her misery instantly. I knew there was not such a thing as a mercy killing, but she wouldn't have stopped, and there's nothing more I could have done to make her stop. Didn't mean I couldn't find a way to get it done.

Two words: rubber rounds.

She was not about to get off that easily.

I checked her body to make sure she was still breathing, moving over to Natasha and sajira to get the zip cuffs off them and take the tape off their mouths. As much as she didn't want to show her gratitude, sajira kissed me deep, quickly disengaging when she realized what she was doing.

She turned red from the blushing over her outward display of affection, lowering her eyes as she remembered her protocol. "Sir, please forgive me for doing that. i was scared that i might die, but seeing You helped keep me calm. Why did she take us like that? What did we do to her?"

"I'll have your Daddy explain after we get the two of you checked out at the hospital, sajira." I patted her hand to ease her emotional state. She gave up a weak smile, realizing that her body was going into mild shock from the experience. Luckily, the EMTs were entering the room to check on them. "I'm glad I was able to get to you two before anything horrible happened."

"Thank You, Sir, i hope i will be allowed to find a way to repay you for saving us."

"I'm sure we'll find some way to get that taken care of. For now, let the paramedics check you out. I'll call your Daddy and let Him know you're okay."

Once they attended to sajira, I turned my attention to the property that belonged to me. "Are you okay, baby?"

"Yes, my Sir, although I didn't have this in mind when I said I had a fetish for predicament bondage." Listening to her make jokes in light of the tense situation was a welcome relief. It was also her defense mechanism for dealing with high-stress situations. "Thank You for coming to get me. I knew You would."

"I didn't have much of a choice; your sis would have killed Me if I didn't." I slipped a kiss over her lips as we awaited the EMTs to check her out and the police officers to interview me on what happened. "There was nothing on this planet that would have stopped Me from coming for you…nothing."

TWENTY-FOUR

I did what I could to relax as much as I could over the next day so I could prepare for the other case. With the other case now over except for the paperwork, I felt the need to work through some of the particulars of the Ashton assault. I couldn't explain it, but it seemed like there was something I was missing, and it was gnawing at me to no end.

I listened to the audio of the interrogation of sirius, trying to find as many clues as I could that would open this thing up and give me an idea of whatever was throwing things off.

I slammed my hand against the desk in frustration as my cell phone rang at nearly the same instant. I didn't have to guess who it was; Ramesses had been trying to contact me all morning, but I'd been ignoring the calls for the simple fact that I didn't have any answers for him as of yet.

The calls wouldn't cease until I answered, so I put myself out of my own misery and put on the best professional voice I could, regardless of how I felt. "Yes, Sir, what can I do for you?"

Ramesses didn't flinch on his first question. "I know you're ignoring my calls, partner, but I didn't want you obsessing over this case when the answer might be sitting in front of you."

I was ready to spit nails when he said that. He tended to see things from an angle altogether differently than anyone else, and it worked my nerves. I was supposed to be the grizzled veteran, but sometimes I wondered if I was the rookie at times with some of these cases. "Enlighten me, Sir. I have got to hear what you have to say on this."

He couldn't stop laughing when he heard me say that. After he took a minute to calm himself, he got dead serious in seconds. "Okay, now that the jokes are out of the way, what if there was a third person involved who might have been pulling the strings the entire time? We know Segal is in on it, but he's not that smart to be able to pull this off by himself. Who would be the plant that was placed in plain sight?"

Was he serious right now? I needed to scream in that moment. He was right; there were more than a few people pulling the strings, and they did so much to try to not seem like they were together that it couldn't have been more obvious. We were so focused on one person that the others quietly worked behind the scenes in other capacities, trying their best to put an innocent man behind bars.

The fucked-up part was, he was willing to do it for money, and the love of a woman who had no more interest in him than she would the Hunchback of Notre Dame. Until he found out how long he would have to wait to claim both. It was the perfect cover, and I was really pissed that I didn't sniff it out sooner, but the other case screwed with my focus.

"Please tell me that you figured this out in the past few hours or so and you weren't torturing me with this bullshit?"

"You should know me by now, Dom. I don't torture anyone except my girls, and they don't always enjoy it when it happens." His voice never wavered, nor did he hesitate in anything he was telling me. That's how I knew he was going to drop the hammer. "To answer your question, no, I didn't figure it out until I did some digging of the other players involved in the situation and what they hoped to gain. You might need to get down there and stop Sharpe from making a mistake that's going to cost him a few years down the road."

"How am I supposed to do that? They have a confession already."

"I'll have the information you need to change their minds by the time you get in the truck. I haven't steered you wrong yet, young'un, so trust me when I say I got you."

I jumped in the truck and headed downtown as quickly as I could. Once he was in my ear, explaining what he'd found out through his kink-related sources, I was even more convinced that a trap needed to be set for the two that thought they'd gotten away with this shit.

If I played this right, and I could get Sharpe involved, I could kill two birds with one stone, which was exactly what I'd set out to do in the first place.

TWENTY-FIVE

I couldn't get to the precinct fast enough.

I popped out of the truck and rushed inside the building, doing my best to not draw too much attention to myself. The power walk was enough to let folks know there was more to the situation than what I might have tried not to let on.

Sharpe listened to everything I had to say to him, including the angle that Ramesses came up with and the information he had to probably shut everything down, and he had to take a seat for a minute.

Ever the logical mind, he still had facts to stipulate and questions to ask. He reminded me too much of my business partner. "We have a confession. The victim was recovered. Why are we revisiting this again?"

It was an uphill battle, but I needed Sharpe to believe me when I said there was something wrong about the whole confession that sirius signed off on. I was convinced there was more to this than a man who was obsessed with the object of his desire.

He was obsessed with someone, but it wasn't who we originally thought it was.

I needed time to gather the proof before they took this to arraignment and trial.

"Look, Sharpe, I don't know how I can tell you this without sounding crazy, but something doesn't add up here. It's too clean, and Segal was the one who helped connect the dots, too? Something doesn't smell funny to you, bruh?"

Sharpe looked like he wanted to strangle me, but my track record spoke for itself, both with and away from the department. My detective work managed to keep innocent men from getting caught up in the system. It wasn't exactly noble work, but I had this overly developed sense of getting shit right the first time.

"So, what do you suggest we do, huh? The only person that might be able to have a clue in hell of what to tell us is still in a coma."

"I understand that, but there's something that we're missing, I can feel it. The information Ramesses had is compelling on top of that. It's enough to reopen this thing and figure out if we have the right man." I did as best I could to quickly present my case as I could without boring the man. "He's way too willing to take the heat for something that could put him away for the next ten to fifteen. Give me a shot at him; let me see if I can get him to crack. If I can't, then he's signed his own sentence."

It was a long shot, but I wouldn't be able to sleep knowing that I didn't exhaust every possible angle. This dude was not built for that life; the real criminals would eat him alive before he got out of prison, if they didn't kill him first.

Sharpe was skeptical; thankfully, I still had authorization from the DA's office to be able to interrogate suspects, something that I usually tried to avoid doing unless the circumstances made it absolutely necessary. This was definitely a textbook definition of that very circumstance. "Do me a favor; when you light him up, don't make it look bad, you feel me?"

He called for one of the detention officers to get sirius from the holding cell. The minute he sat down in the interrogation room, he immediately got agitated. "Why am I back in here? I gave you what you wanted. What do you want to do now, torture me?"

I walked through the door, locking eyes with him as soon as I sat down. He took one look in my eyes and instantly his demeanor changed. "Sir, please forgive me, i wasn't aware You needed to speak with me. What questions do You have that i can answer for You?"

"you have Me at a disadvantage; have we met before?"

"No, Sir, we haven't, but i have known of You for a long time, through mutual acquaintances. i have also served Lady Neferterri on occasion and Mistress Lohyna." He looked nearly in awe of me for some reason, and I couldn't figure out where the reverence came from. Outside of my work through the firm, I hadn't earned much of anything to get the "rock star" treatment.

He mentioned Lohyna's name and the next thing I knew, I heard a knock on the window. "Excuse me a moment."

When I got inside the observation room, there was a concerned look on Sharpe's face. I wasn't sure what to think of it until he showed me paperwork and shook his head. "We just got the fax from our forensic accountants just now. Lohyna has an account that was just wired one hundred thousand over the last two days. You might have been right; he's covering for someone, could it have been Lohyna since he's served her before?"

"Did it say where the transfers came from?" I wasn't ready to bury Lohyna yet; nothing and no one were ever what they seemed. I'd learned that over the past eighteen months. "Where did the money come from? Lohyna isn't exactly rubbing elbows with Atlanta's high society and such."

A grin popped across Sharpe's face, like he knew I would like the answer to that question. "Neal Segal."

I felt like I'd won the lottery. "Tell me he wasn't *that* fucking sloppy? Oh, he's so fucked. I feel like I need to be the one to arrest him."

"Niki is requesting an arrest warrant as we speak." Sharpe took the paperwork back from me before he nodded in sirius's direction. "Until we can get him in the box, there might be a need to connect the dots and make this all work. Since he's already gushing for you more than he has for anyone else, maybe you can get him to bust this case open."

He had a point, and this was one of those times where I needed to use the advantage I had to do what needed to be done.

I walked back into the room, looking straight through him with this intense expression on my face. He looked a little spooked, like he might have known I was on to something. Before I could speak one word, he started tapping his fingers on the table, avoiding eye contact the best way he could, anything but the prospect of facing me.

"Sir, i'm scared. i thought i could go through with it, but i can't anymore. It's not worth it." The flood gates were opened and I hadn't had a chance to really even go into my shtick. "i gave the information to create Lohyna's account to someone i thought i could trust. i was in love with her; she said that if i confessed, i would be able to qualify under the First Offender laws and maybe get a suspended sentence as long as diamante didn't die."

"Who was the person you thought you could trust? Who was she?" This situation began to turn in a direction that I didn't expect, but the wild part was that once he painted himself into a corner, it all made sense.

He confirmed Ramesses's suspicions with the mention of one name. "Serena Ashton."

Wait a damned minute? He couldn't be talking about her, could he?

The more I thought about it over the next few moments, the more it made sense. She was the one that he was obsessed over, she was the one who waited long enough to figure out when to even report her missing, and went through back channels to report her missing. Considering she didn't know whom to contact, she had to be told by someone to come find me and me only.

The look in his eyes lent themselves to the severity of the situation. If he was willing to burn her and anyone else to preserve his freedom, it could be that he was lying to cover himself, too.

I needed more before I could be convinced. "And how do you know Serena?"

"she used to serve Kraven at one point in time, and i met her at his house for a private party. We fell for each other that night and we were together for a while before Kraven released her from service." sirius tried his best to wipe away tears as he began to realize how badly he'd been played. "She came to me one night after we were intimate one night, told me that she knew who replaced her, and she wanted her out of the way, badly."

"How do you figure into this scenario, sirius? Tell me what happened to diamante, were you the one who roughed her up?"

"i never touched her, Sir; i swear that i didn't. That night, Serena called me and told me where i could find diamante. When i got to where she was, she was beaten up badly. i couldn't let her die, Sir. i picked her up and put her in my car and drove her to Emory; my sister works there, and i knew she would cover for me and try to take care of her."

"Who is your sister? Wait a minute, never mind, I think I already know." My mind went back to the charge nurse who had all the clout and power when she took us to Kendyl's room to begin with. "So, Serena had a hand in this, too, right?"

"Yes, Sir. i thought she loved me. i can't believe i almost gave up my freedom for her. And for what? A measly hundred grand? What was i thinking?"

"Did you realize that you almost helped a woman kill her sister, dude?" I couldn't resist rubbing it in. He needed to know how deep this shit went. "I mean, I get it; sometimes you think you got it figured out, especially when they tell you all the right things. You knew what you were thinking, but you weren't ready to do hard time, were you?"

I sat there watching as he put his head in his hands and tried his best to look like he hadn't fallen victim to a pretty face, when the reality of his acts slapped him hard across the mouth. It was very hard not to fall victim to someone who had you wide open. If someone even tried to sound like they had never been made a fool of, they'd never been in love before.

The fact that he was able to come to his senses and not put himself in a bad position should've been a prideful moment for him. It wasn't going to be easy to recover from this, but at least he had his freedom. That's something no one should ever give up for anyone they weren't married to or related to, and even then I would question their sanity.

"You thought you were in love, man. It makes fools of us all." I rose from the table and headed for the door. "I'll let Sharpe know that you need to be processed out. There's no need to hold you any longer."

"Thank You, Sir, i really appreciate it." The tears flowed freely as he realized that he was off the hook. He motioned for me to come over to him, leaning me close so I would be the only one to hear what he had to say. "i still have something that i think You might be able to use, in case Serena tries to pin this all on Kraven. She's not about to get away with this like her hands weren't dirty in all this."

Listening to him explain what Serena did to her sister was enough for me to vomit. All this over something so petty? And the things she did to get away with it was enough to have me steaming mad.

She was going to pay, and she was going to pay dearly.

I got back into the observation room, and Sharpe had some more good news for me. "Kendyl is awake, and according to the nurse we were dealing with, she wants to talk to us."

🔫🔫🔫

"Follow me, gentlemen; she's awake and alert, which is interesting to say the least. Usually the speech patterns are the last to come into clarity, but she's a strong girl."

We walked with Kim to Kendyl's room, and sure enough, she was watching television and laughing at the ratchetness on the screen. I could relate; I needed something to take my mind off my troubles, too. Not that I watched nonsense like that on the regular, but it was a necessary evil, so it didn't bother me in the slightest.

Kim entered into the room first to introduce us to her. "Ms. Ashton, these are the gentlemen I was telling you came to see you a couple of days ago. This is Detective Sharpe and Detective Law."

"Hello." She smiled at Sharpe, but she gave me a curious look of recognition. "i know You; my former Sir doesn't like You very much. It makes this easier to do knowing that You're helping with this case. Poetic justice, in a sense."

I almost wanted to laugh, but I kept my head for the sake of the conversation we were about to have with her. Sharpe shook his head; I didn't think he realized how small the kink community was in the different cities throughout the country.

"It would be a bit of poetic justice indeed, Ms. Ashton." Sharpe began working through the evidence in his head to figure out what to ask first. "The first question would be if you remember what happened to you?"

"How could i forget?" Kendyl sat up in bed for a moment, taking a sip of the juice on her tray. At first it looked like she was going to tear up as she recollected the events of that night, but the switch went off in her head and her face was expressionless. "My sister tried to kill me."

"Wait a minute, how did you know your sister tried to kill you?"

"The person who was with her called her by her name, that's how." Kendyl looked directly at us, nearly sounding deadpan with her response. "He called her by her name, which pissed her off, to say the least. I actually played dead to keep them from beating me any more than they already had. The other guy supposedly checked my pulse and couldn't find anything, so she told him to get rid of the body. By then, I'd blacked out. When I woke up, I was here at the hospital."

"Well, sounds like we have a positive ID of the real suspect." Sharpe looked over at me, watching me shake my head. It wasn't a complete identification; the other man she was referring to was the last piece of the puzzle. He pressed Kendyl for one last question. "Was the other man your former Sir, Kendyl?"

"Yes, it was." Kendyl closed her eyes and breathed deeply, trying to realize the depths of the treachery against her. Her eyes found me the minute she opened them. "Kraven i expected this from; His words to me one day a while back was, 'I drop bitches, they don't drop Me.' i should have been more careful, should have kept my head and told someone that i was dealing with Him, but He was so insistent on being private, and at the time i was really into Him. He's a psychopath, Sir; He needs to be put away. i should have listened to my Mistress."

I'm going to bury him for good. She gave me the information I needed. Conspiracy to commit attempted murder would fit nicely on Kraven's smug ass. This couldn't have gone any better. The only thing that was left was the big reveal to both of them when we had them brought in and arrested.

I walked over and kissed her palm, a smile crossing my face as I got the chance to tell her the news I knew she wanted to hear. "I'll be sure to let your Mistress know you're here. I'm sure She'll be thrilled to know you're alive and well."

"i miss Her so much. Yes, please let Her know; i can't wait to see Her."

As we headed out of the hospital, Sharpe continued to muse over what he'd witnessed. "I have a feeling that I need to learn a thing or two about this community you are a part of. I have a feeling it's going to be an eye-opening experience, and it might help me moving forward, if we keep working these types of cases."

"Yeah, it might help on a lot of fronts, bruh. It just might help indeed. Now, let's take out the trash."

TWENTY-SIX

Consider tonight's series of unfortunate events a prime case of "dueling banjos."

This shit was so hilarious, I wouldn't have believed it if someone sat me down and told me about it.

I had to walk between two observation rooms to watch the drama unfold, but it was must-see drama that had to be viewed. Anything else would have been uncivilized!

Serena was in one room being interrogated by Niki, while Kraven was in the other room being interrogated by Sharpe. Both had the evidence to put each of their respective suspects away, but it was fun to watch the two of them squirm as they each were being put through the rigors of the interview. It was times like this when I missed being in the box, the intensity of it all. The only thing I could do now was watch and enjoy the show.

"Why in the hell am I here? I thought your people already had the suspect in custody?" I heard Kraven through the speakers, demanding to be told what was going on with him and why he was arrested. "There's no way in hell that I could be arrested. Where's my lawyer?"

"He'll be here shortly, Mr. Segal, and until he shows up, I wanted to remind you of your rights again, to make sure that you understand them before you start saying anything more." Sharpe knew Kraven was trying to bait him; I warned him about that the minute the arrest warrants were issued. It was entertaining hearing about how he got popped at his house, and watching him squirm was the stuff of legend. "Would you like for me to read you your rights again, so we're clear?"

"You don't have to do a goddamned thing for me except let me out of this room and let me go about my business." Kraven was really animated and pissed! It was a damn shame all of that bravado would go to waste. "I swear, I'm gonna have your job by the time we're done here."

The first thing Sharpe dropped on the table top was a stack of papers, which housed the information that sirius had provided for us. It was the wire transfers from Kraven's account to Lohyna's "new" account, not even two weeks old. He directed Kraven to read the contents of the paperwork, studying his face as the reality of the situation began to sink in.

Gotcha, you sick son of a bitch.

"Now that I have your attention, Mr. Segal, can you explain how you were able to open an account in your ex-wife's name, without her consent or signature, and wire money into that account from an offshore bank account?" Sharpe wanted to laugh at how panicked Kraven looked at that moment, and I was waiting for the exact timing when Kraven would earn his scene name and turn into a turncoat against his co-conspirator.

"Wait a minute, you got this all wrong, detective. I didn't open this account; it was my submissive, Serena, who did this. I swear it! It was her idea to get rid of her sister after she dumped me to be with my ex." The words came fast and heavy from Kraven, each one putting the nail in his coffin without him even realizing it. He should have waited for his lawyer; it shouldn't have taken some-thing so simple to make him crack. "Don't you get it? I would never have laid a finger on heaven, even though she dumped me. Why would I even bother; I had her sister, and I have her again now."

"That's not what the victim stated, sir. In fact, she's willing to testify that you were there with her during the commission of the crime. You're going down, sir; your best bet is to admit to it so we can at least try to find some way to get the DA's office to grant you some leniency."

Sharpe was about to dig in deep, but I wanted to see what was going on with Niki and Serena. I didn't want to miss out on the fun over there, either.

Sure enough, by the time I got into the other observation room to pick up on the action, my girl was damn near waist-deep putting Serena away. "What sick mind does something like this to her own flesh and blood?"

"First of all, if any of you idiots had been paying attention, you'd realize that she's not my sister; she's my half-sister, thanks to my father marrying that woman after my mom passed away." Serena was as hot as Kraven was in the other room. "Secondly, I didn't do anything to her, fuck you very much."

"Yeah, that's what you're saying now, and I beg to differ, seriously. You're a slick one, all right, and you had my detectives believing that you cared about her, too? I should go ahead and have aggravated assault charges pinned on you and ask for the maximum. That should have you on ice for the next twenty years or so." Niki was using the sharp knives on her, slicing as deeply as she could. "We know your Sir was with you when you both tried to kill your sister. It's only a matter of time before the one who sings first gets the best deal. So, do you want to be the bird that sings, or are you going to let your Sir throw you under the bus to save his own neck?"

"My Sir would not do anything of the sort. He loves me too much to let me burn like that." Serena seemed defiant to the very end. They deserved each other as far as I was concerned. "I already know what you're trying to do, but it won't work; you don't have anything to hold me here."

"Oh, you don't think we do? Well, how about I show you what we don't have and let you make the final call over what you think we do and don't have, okay?"

Once the evidence got dropped in her lap of what we knew, including the fact that her sister was conscious and talking, her eyes widened and she was ready to sing a different tune. "It was his idea! He was pissed about her leaving him and he knew I was still salty about being dumped for her. He said we could be together if I did this for him."

"So, you sold out your sister—excuse me, half-sister—for some dick? And not just any dick, some old, decrepit, shriveled-up limp shit, too." Niki was laying it on thick, scoffing as she tried to wrap her head around the concept. "Damn, I could see if it was my Sir, as fine as he is, but all I can say is wow. He must have put it on you, girl."

"Oh, I get it, you're in the scene, too, huh? I should have known by the way you move and talk that you were. Kraven is more of a man than your Sir could ever be, whoever the fuck he is. Bitches don't leave him; he leaves bitches and moves on to the next."

"Meanwhile, you go crawling back to that sad sack of shit at the first sign of his needing you, and you happily try to kill someone you have negative feelings about, only to mess that up." She waited as Serena's lips formed an "O." "Yeah, your sister is awake; she just came out of her coma. My detectives finished talking to her before we had you and your Sir arrested. I think you might want to see about your lawyer right about now."

Checkmate in interrogation room two.

Now that that was over and done, I ran over to the other room to catch up on what I missed. I hadn't gotten in there for a few minutes when I heard Kraven almost lose it.

"This is all circumstantial evidence and hearsay! I know heaven isn't alive; I checked her pulse myself!"

I kept my mouth shut. I wanted Sharpe to really play up the comedy in this particular series of exchanges between him and Kraven, but to his credit, he kept it on the level, trying to be as professional as he possibly could.

He rose from his chair, doing as much as he could to keep whatever laughs he had pent up until he left the room. He shook his head, leaving a confused suspect wondering why he looked so pitifully at him.

"What the fuck is your problem? The fuck do you find so funny?" Kraven's scowl was met with indifference as Sharpe did his best to keep a straight face as he laid the groundwork for what exactly Kraven had done to really put himself in such a fucked-up position that even God himself couldn't get him out of this mess.

"I'll tell you what you've done, since you seem to think that you have done nothing wrong. You've just admitted to being at the scene of the crime, and then you admitted to touching the victim to check her vital signs. Damn, are you sure you don't want to wait for your lawyer? This isn't looking good for you at all."

"None of this will hold up in court! You coerced me into admitting guilt! My lawyer will have a field day with this!" Kraven was livid at this point, doing his best to sound like those armchair lawyers.

As much as he tried to sound defiant and belligerent with the words coming out of his mouth, he forgot one small detail.

Sharpe must have felt like he was in some wild alternate universe or something; confessions didn't come this easy. He reminded Kraven of that detail he missed on the way out of the door. "I'll tell you what, let me leave you to your devices for a moment until your lawyer gets here, and we can start all over again, okay? And please remember, before you decide to tell your attorney that you were coerced, this was all on audio and video, and that I advised you of your right to remain silent before you started flapping off at the mouth."

I waited for Sharpe to come out as Niki came into the room almost simultaneously. I should have been professional about my reaction, but the truth was I was having a hard time standing up from the laughter that I felt from my stomach. "God, don't you wish they were all that damn easy?"

"I had to find some way to get out of there, Law. He was so convinced we didn't have anything on him that he was willing to insult me to the moon and back." Sharpe cracked a smile as he turned to Niki. "So, what did you get out of his...submissive, right?"

"Right...look at you, trying to figure out the ins and outs of things," Niki replied. "Serena said she was the one who actually first struck Kendyl, but she didn't land the blow that rendered her unconscious. I can still make aggravated assault stick, even though there was an intent to murder. They simply weren't able to finish the job, for whatever reason."

"So, are these cases open and shut, for the most part, now?" I had to ask the question more for clarity to tell my partner than for anything else. Even a blind man could see these two were ready to be sliced and prepared for slaughter. "Honestly, I think I deserve to let my partner know that the case is handled and done, and that our issues with Mr. Segal are over with now."

"Yes, my Sir, You can do exactly that." Niki beamed as she kissed me on the cheek. "Please give them my best, too, all right? i feel like i need to see them soon anyway; it's been too long since You took us to see them."

I laughed at her being slick with her mouth, knowing I couldn't really admonish her in front of Sharpe. I simply nodded and headed out of the door to deliver the good news to Ramesses and put these cases to bed.

EPILOGUE

"I'm sorry to have to be the one to tell you this, sir. We were able to find the persons behind your daughter's assault."

This was never the easiest thing to go through, having to explain to the victim's family what actually happened once things were sorted out. With crimes like this, you almost always want it to be committed by a complete stranger. From a cathartic sense, it helps the healing process speed up, if that had any roots in logical thought.

To have to explain to Mr. Ashton that his firstborn was one of the persons responsible for the assault and near death of his youngest—and her sister, at that—I was better off telling him that Kraven was behind it. Considering his past and his thoughts on interracial relationships, I wasn't sure which would hurt worse.

To have Mr. Ashton cut me off before I could get to the point to where I could explain the details to him was disorienting, to say the least. He looked relieved and carefree, like he was going to move on to the next issue that he needed to see about.

"That's wonderful, detective. Thank you for being able to get this done so quickly and keeping things out of the public eye," Mr. Ashton said as he extended his hand out to shake mine. "We're relieved that Kendyl is alive and safe now, and that the persons responsible will be held accountable."

I was a bit confused that he didn't want to know what happened.

Usually, parents want to know the particulars, especially when the arraignment hearing would be, so they could attend to ensure justice was served. "Forgive me, sir, but I'm a bit curious; aren't you curious about the particulars of the hearing?"

Mr. Ashton gave me a curious look, putting me further in an awkward position as to what direction to take this conversation. He didn't blink when he responded about as matter-of-factly as I'd ever heard him. "Son, let me tell you something; sometimes when it comes to those that you care about most, they find a way to disappoint you in such a way that you can no longer really put your heart out on the line anymore. It might sound harsh, but when you've done your all for your children and they continue to do things that you know they shouldn't and it takes them down a path that you cannot save them from, you have to let them fall and pick up the pieces of their own mess."

I thought I was hearing things. I wasn't a parent; not sure if I would ever be, either. Hearing him talk like that—like the end of the proverbial rope had been reached—was something that was foreign to me. I had done some stupid shit as a teenager, but never once did my parents ever turn their backs on me.

The flip side of the coin was that I wasn't the offspring of a Civil Rights legend, either. The standard that was expected must have been insane growing up in that house. In essence, he was disowning and disavowing any knowledge that he had more than one child, and as much as I wanted to act like that didn't hurt, it did.

"Well, sir, I hope that your other daughter is on the mend and that she is able to get back to being what she has been before this unfortunate circumstance. I'll bid you good night, and please give my best to your wife."

I couldn't get out of that house fast enough. He was a real piece of work; he inadvertently ruined my image of an icon. Sometimes, that's what happened when you put extraordinary men on a pedestal based on their actions; once you get a chance to get up close and personal, you see they're as ordinary as you are, they simply rose to extraordinary actions for extraordinary circumstances.

I clicked on the CD player, listening to my dude T.I., rocking "Memories Back Then" to clear my mind from the madness I'd just dealt with, and for the first time, I actually had to think about the losses I took with these last cases.

Losing Tori. Almost losing Ty, Natasha and sajira. If he didn't have those tracking chips implanted in sajira, things could have turned out a lot worse than they did. I couldn't be that sloppy again. The last thing I needed was to lose either one of the girls. I didn't think I could handle that.

"I know you're in the midst of a short vacation, partner, but I think there's something you might need to be brought up to speed on."

I was getting a bit perturbed about the interruptions that my business partner tended to make at some of the more inopportune times in my life. It cost to be the boss, and the clock was not always punched out like a regular worker, but I had hoped to have a little time to myself while enjoying my girls in the French Riviera.

Yeah, I know, it was a bit extravagant for a four-day junket, but it was a needed break outside the States for a change. The Caribbean was becoming a bore, and I wanted somewhere new to cross off the travel bucket list I had in my head. Bringing Natasha and Niki along was simply icing on the cake.

I made a mental note to turn off the international roaming on my phone the next time I traveled out of the country.

"You know, you have this penchant ability to find me at times that I don't want to be disturbed, Sir." I didn't care about mincing words, and I wasn't about to sugarcoat anything at the given moment. Natasha was still healing from the incident that Veronica put her through, and I was almost healed from my injuries from dealing with Karrion. "But since the girls are off getting pampered for a few, I have time to talk. So, what's so important that you had to get at me from across the pond?"

There was a slight pause from Ramesses that I wasn't sure I wanted to feel comfortable about. He sighed, resigning himself to explain in as little wording as possible the reason for his call. "There was another sexual assault and murder, this time at one of the other compounds. This one's taking us to D.C., bruh. Do not pass Atlanta on the way back; I'll meet you in Alexandria."

I was still at loss and having a failure to understand what was going on. He could have handled that with the authorities in Virginia, where Thebes was located. Besides, we didn't have any law enforcement connections that I was familiar with enough to even feel like working a case up that way. He was withholding information, as usual. "So, don't keep me in suspense, Sir; what's the reason that I need to meet you in Virginia?"

The answer he gave was enough to stop me in my tracks. "Ayanna's been murdered, partner. It looks bad, too; I'm already en route as we're speaking, so I can see what the hell happened at Thebes."

My world stopped. I remembered Ayanna saying she was taking a trip up that way to visit some friends, but for Ramesses to say that it was a murder and rape…that was more than I could handle at that moment.

The fact that it happened inside the compound was even more disturbing.

"I'll be on the first thing smoking in the morning, Sir." I straightened up in my chair, determined to clear my mind from my vacation haze. "I'll meet you at Thebes."

"Good man. I'll see you there." Ramesses cleared his throat like he had one more thing to say. I almost wished he hadn't said it. "Oh, and while we're there, we're going to have to handle some business with the Council. That's all I can say for now, but I will bring you up to speed when you get Stateside. See you tomorrow, Sir, and rest well. You're going to need it."

ABOUT THE AUTHOR

Known for his mind-twisting plots and unique prose, Shakir Rashaan rolled onto the literary scene as a contributing writer to Z-Rated: Chocolate Flava 3 in 2012. His raw, vivid, and uncut writing style captured the attention of the Queen of Erotica herself, Zane. A year later, Rashaan made his debut with *The Awakening*, opening to rave reviews and a "recommended read" accolade in *USA Today*'s "Happy Ever After" literary blog. The follow-up in the *Nubian Underworld* series, *Legacy*, has garnered even more success, and its third installment, *Tempest*, picked up yet another "recommended read" from *USA Today*'s "HEA" blog, making the series one of the most unique in the erotica genre.

Reckoning is the third of the *Kink, P.I.* series, and along with the first two installments, *Obsession* and *Deception*, they have added another exciting series to the mystery genre. A few new projects are also being developed under the pen name, P.K. Rashaan. With his prolific writing prowess and openness on his social media platforms, Rashaan has plans to be a mainstay within the erotica genre and beyond.

Shakir is a Phoenix, earning his Bachelor of Science degree in Criminal Justice/Communications from the University of Phoenix. He currently resides in suburban Atlanta with his wife and two children.

Follow the author on social media, or contact him.
Twitter: http://twitter.com/ShakirRashaan
Facebook: http://www.facebook.com/Shakir.Rashaan
Instagram: http://instagram.com/ShakirRashaan
Email: shakir@shakirrashaan.com
Blog: http://www.medium.com/@ShakirRashaan

WE'RE GLAD YOU ENJOYED "RECKONING,"
BOOK THREE IN THE "KINK, P.I." SERIES.
IF YOU WANT TO KNOW HOW DOM AND KANE
GOT STARTED BE SURE TO CHECK OUT

OBSESSION

THE KINK, P.I. SERIES: BOOK 1

BY SHAKIR RASHAAN
AVAILABLE FROM STREBOR BOOKS

ONE

Hate me or love me, I get results…

I'm damn good at what I do. Sure, I bent the rules a little bit, but what cop hadn't? But I was never…I repeat, never…dirty. Ask any of my old partners and they'd tell you that for a fact.

I enjoyed the rigors of the job, the satisfaction of getting the bad guys off the streets, all of that. When I was promoted to detective, the only thing that changed was the clothes that I wore and the trademark fedora that the detectives wore to distinguish themselves from the beat patrol. I was on the fast track to doing some really big things, and I probably would have gotten them done, too.

The funniest thing about setting goals and planning out the future is the old cliché: "life is what happens to you while you're busy making plans."

Life was what happened to me when my childhood partner-in-crime came calling and said the words that would alter my future forever. "I got something for you, bruh. This is going to be a game-changer, I promise you." I was skeptical at first, if I was honest with myself, so I told him I would think about it and get back to him.

He gave me twenty-four hours.

By the time he showed me the capital he had at his disposal to keep me happy and pull me away from APD, I jumped at his proposal with the speed of a Shinkansen bullet train. That's what I did a year ago, and I haven't looked back since.

He and I go way back. In fact, we were damn near partners on the force together, until he decided to start doing his photography thing and began to blow up. We went our separate ways after that. I never held a grudge against him about it, though. The way I saw it, things had a funny way of working themselves out, and he always said he would find a way to get me out of APD before he felt he had to bury me.

Oh, by the way, the name's Law, Dominic Law, but my now business partner Ramesses liked to refer to me by my nickname, Dom. He called me that when we were in high school and the nickname kinda stuck. But now, instead of Detective Law of the Atlanta Police Department, you could call me by a different moniker: Private Investigator. I still answer to Detective Law, of course, but the APD part was no longer necessary.

Actually, it's more than that: I ran the P.I. business, yes, but I was also the head of Ramesses's security detail at NEBU and Neferterri's security detail at her club, Liquid Paradise. All in all, they kept me quite busy with everything that went on.

But that's not all. Thanks to Ramesses's father's connections all over the city, I picked up a lot of cases that the various P.D.s couldn't always deem high priority, especially when sometimes the cases weren't always "normal" by mainstream standards. After a while, I developed the reputation as the "Kink Detective," which had its share of perks, at least from a financial perspective. When the occasion called for it, I could be brought in on a consult for the more unusual sex crimes that needed my "specific expertise." A lot of the crimes were kink-related, coincidentally, and I found myself immersed deep inside the BDSM and Fetish community. It wasn't like I wasn't already into the shit to begin with; I could thank Ramesses and Amenhotep for that. I honestly didn't think that I wanted to be *that* deep, but when you saw how women like Ramesses's and Neferterri's submissives and the slaves at NEBU treated a neophyte Dominant like me, it was very hard to resist learning how to get that same treatment.

Oh, and so we're clear, my boy had damn near converted me. My only problem, as he saw it, was that I was the new "meat" on the scene. I was a heterosexual black man and my best friend—who was mentoring me, by the way—happened to be one of the power players in the Atlanta BDSM community, and damn near at the top of the food chain within the black BDSM community. The women on the scene drooled over me once they found out I was a cop at one point in time.

So, what was the problem, you were wondering?

Technically there was no problem, unless you included an ex-wife that happened to be into the same thing that I, when we were married, could really never be a part of, due to the nature of my occupation, as a problem. Even though law enforcement made strides in their understanding recently, fifteen years ago when I was coming out of the Academy, there was no way I could be able to be a cop in the Deep South and try to be discreet doing "kinky shit."

In fact, it's one of the "irreconcilable differences" she listed when she filed for divorce a few years ago. Now, not only was I a newbie in the community, but I had to occasionally run into her at munches or at NEBU when a larger community function was going on. Talk about awkward?

I'd dwell on this some more, but you probably couldn't care less. If you're like most Americans, you're simply going to lump me into that collection of oddballs that you thought of as "the strange people." Well, with the recent popularity of what Ramesses called "that godforsaken movie," maybe there might not be such a rush to judgment anymore, but I'd been known to be wrong before.

I was one of the popular people at one of the local munches on the west side. Oh, yeah, that's right, I'm assuming that you knew the "strange person" jargon, so let me get you caught up to speed a bit in case you didn't. A munch was short for a "meet and lunch" and that was the proper, and original, term for a gathering of people in the bondage, dominance and sadomasochism lifestyle, better known by the umbrella term of BDSM. And while we're at it, take a minute to add Leather to your mental label for me. Go ahead, I'll wait. You would be wrong, though. Not everyone into BDSM, or the lifestyle as we called it, was a leather-clad "freak." A lot of us were, including Ramesses and Amenhotep, I'll grant you, but not all of us…at least, not me.

It's not like that wouldn't stop Ramesses, though. To let him tell it, we'd have a plethora of issues to deal with now that the movie had rekindled the fervor of all the wannabes that thought that the "talented" Mr. Grey was hanging out at any of the three other dungeons in addition to NEBU. Trust me, if that dude, or any resemblance or copycat of him, showed up at the security checkpoint, I'd probably have him turned around and revoke his membership based on the illegitimacy of his "dominance" alone.

Look at me, I'm sounding like Ramesses again. Damn it.

Well, he had me convinced, but I had no intentions of sounding like a damn tape recorder, either.

Anyway, munches varied in tone. It's all to do with the people involved. The West Atlanta munch was mostly made up of the well-educated and well-employed, so the only difference between one of our gatherings and a meeting of your local Kiwanis Club was...well, damned if I knew.

The tone was set by the group leaders—and with this particular munch, it was Ramesses, Neferterri and Mistress Sinsual—and generally the folks who had been around the longest. People also dressed casually: blue jeans, dresses, skirts and blouses, clean sneakers, and even the occasional suit.

The reason I was explaining all of this to you in detail was so you could understand why I wasn't surprised when peaches sat down across from me. Well, that's not entirely accurate; I was surprised, but she didn't need to know the reason why. Of course, peaches was not her real name. Let me rephrase that: peaches was her real name in the sense that it's the only one she'd answer to because it's the name her Master gave her.

Don't worry about understanding everything; just keep up with me and Ramesses and let the otherness sort of wash over you like a golden shower.

Sorry, I couldn't resist.

The real reason I was surprised to see peaches here, much less anywhere outside of Inner Sanctum, one of the other local dungeons I mentioned, especially without her "beloved Master." The West Atlanta munch was a place for people to socialize among other libertines, and Lord Aris and his harem weren't really capable of getting outside and into the community. He thought it was a waste of time, except to collect more girls for his personal enjoyment. Ramesses and his mentor, Amenhotep, never could stand the guy. Hell, come to think of it, I hadn't run into anyone that really held any affinity for the man, except for the subs that were with him. But, in the interest of keeping harmony in the community, most people tolerated him, so long as he didn't cause any permanent harm to those who kneeled to him.

It wasn't exactly what I would have done if the man ain't worth two dead flies, but I digress.

Upon examining the situation further, I couldn't recall, in my limited experience, ever seeing one of Aris's slaves at a gathering where he wasn't, and that gave me pause. Lord Aris was a controlling asshole, but it seemed that the women who were turned on by him mistook his misogynistic, control-freak attitude and lack of social skills for a commanding air of dominance, and they flocked to him like moths to a flame. He had to beat them off with a stick, which he loved. Hell, what man wouldn't?

However, it still didn't explain how peaches came to be there, and why she was there without the one she kneeled to.

I took another sip of my tea and waited. peaches wanted to talk to me, but the protocol that she's under prohibited her from speaking to a Dominant unless spoken to first. I should have respected that protocol as a courtesy to her Master, but I didn't. In case you hadn't been paying attention, I didn't like Aris much, and he'd been clear and vocal about his disdain for me, if for nothing else, due to my association with Ramesses, nothing more.

So fuck him, and fuck her…I had no time to play bleeding heart games with people I really didn't like all that much.

I let her sit there and make eye contact with the table while I waited for her to decide which was more important: Aris's protocol or her obvious need to talk to me. It was torture for her. Call it a sadistic side of me, but I enjoyed watching her squirm.